DRAGONS OF PROTECTION

BONNIE ELIZABETH

My Big Fat Orange Cat Publishing

Chapter One

When I say dragonflies, most people think of the insect with a long narrow body and speedy little wings. My aunt used to call them sewing needles rather than dragonflies. But here, on Jewel Island, they were tiny little dragons, perhaps the length of my thumb with gossamer wings. Literally, dragon flies, or perhaps dragon-flies. These creatures were, like everything else on Jewel Island, magical.

I'd heard they appear every thirty-eight months and stay for six to nine weeks. This varied depending upon the magical enclave. One enclave had them every eleven months, while another had them about every 75 months. Definitely not normal patterns and I could see no rhyme or reason. They didn't appear more often in southern areas or in the north, nor did they stick around only in spring or summer. They just appeared on a schedule, no matter the season.

While they were cute in the way that kittens and puppies tended to be cute, more dragon than fly, there could be problems. Magic tended to go awry or not work the way it normally did when the dragon-flies showed up.

The first day they'd appeared during my first dragonfly season, I'd nearly burnt myself when a stream of fire came out of my kitchen faucet rather than water. Fortunately, I have quite an affinity for fire magic which gave me some protection. Plus, my beautiful calico cat, Peony, assisted in making sure the magic didn't harm me.

In theory, Jewel Island won't let someone bonded with it be killed, but the island has an interesting definition of being killed. I could inadvertently kill myself by doing something stupid because the island would assume I was getting the result I wanted. Or, if it didn't recognize me, I could die because, apparently, it only cares about people it knows.

I didn't know everything about magic, having only been on the island for about six months. Until my arrival, I'd just been an ordinary fat woman accountant whose husband had decided to trade her in for a younger, thinner model. I'd been out of work, looking for a job, preferably something close to my background in finance. Jewel Island needed an accountant, which was how I came to be here.

So far, I'd learned that everyone has the potential for magic, but you don't actually start using magic until you begin to accept all parts of yourself. It seems the things you are most ashamed of are the parts that provide your magic.

While I'd felt ashamed of being fat for much of my life, trying to make myself smaller, after my divorce, I'd had to come to terms with the fact that I was who I was and part of that was being a fat woman. I didn't need to keep trying to be smaller. I could go out and enjoy the things I loved. If people didn't like my body, that was their problem, not mine. I believe that's why I came into my magic when I did, although I have many other things I feel rather ashamed of, there was nothing else that was so obviously, culturally less than acceptable about me.

Jewel Island is an island in the middle of Lake Michigan, not on any map that I could find, though we are connected to the real world by internet, post office, and the ferry system, not that a non-magical person will see a stop for Jewel if they take the ferry from Michigan to Wisconsin. No one had explained me how the captain would know to stop on Jewel if a magical person wants to go there. Further, if I wanted to leave, the ferry would just appear there on its next run, as if the boat itself was psychic.

If that wasn't confusing enough, if I wanted my sisters to visit me, I'd just need to do the inviting. Like the island gave them special sticker or something that said, "mage family." Every time I got a little comfortable with what I thought the rules of magic were, I'd learn something new.

Bernice, the interim mayor and the woman who taught many of the mages on the island—and we were mages, not witches to differentiate ourselves from the Wiccan community—didn't know how things worked and said no one really did. Ian, my friend who runs the B&B didn't know either and, other than Bernice, he seemed to know the most about the island, at least of the people I was comfortable pestering with questions.

I mean, Lauren, our local librarian probably knew a lot, but she was quieter and self-contained and I didn't know her as well. I mean, Ian had come to my rescue when I'd nearly been killed by Damien Bain, a former resident, and that kind of experience creates a bond between people. Bernice had also helped, although I'd suspected her motives right down to the moment she'd helped save my life.

The day the dead body turned up on the island was not long after tax time, just a few days after the dragon-flies appeared. Ian was in my office wearing one of his plaid vests—this one in blues—over a white shirt and black jeans, along with black plaid high tops. He'd always looked young and when he'd started managing the B&B, he thought the vests made him look older. Black looked professional. The plaid was to remind himself not to be boring. The shoes, he said, were just comfortable.

We were in the reception area of the office, near the desk not far from the front door. It was a quieter time than it had been just a week ago, even. The building smelled of old coffee and the faintest hint of clover, thanks to the dragon-flies. The large picture windows along the entire back wall showcased the lake, which wasn't glassy smooth, holding the occasional white cap wave out in the distance.

Between us and the windows was a sunken living room, very mid-century modern with bench seats and a large fire-place angled towards the room. The HVAC hummed because that morning had been sunny, if not particularly warm. Unfortunately, the large windows meant the poor system worked extra hard all year round, but the view was worth it.

Fog rolled in, which is always a sign that the ferry is coming. The ferry arrives when someone needs to leave or when someone is arriving.

Ian paused in our conversation, frowning.

"That's odd," he said walking closer to the window.

"What is?" I asked.

"I think everyone's here and accounted for, and I'm not expecting anyone at the B&B,"

"Maybe it's someone that didn't make plans ahead of time," I said. Sometimes folks just dropped in and hoped. I knew I wouldn't feel a need to let Ian know if I needed a room. The B&B tended to accommodate everyone.

Magic.

Ian shook his head. "I'd know. It's my link to the B&B. It's not someone coming here. I thought there was earlier, but that feeling passed. I know it's not someone planning on staying with one of the residents. It's weird. I wonder if Bernice has felt it."

I frowned.

"I should go down there," Ian said, meaning he should go down to our little dock where the ferry would stop, the fog hiding the island from eyes that didn't need to see it. Or couldn't. I wasn't sure which.

I grabbed a light jacket and followed him. We'd been planning on doing lunch, my treat for all the times Ian had made sure I'd eaten during tax season. But the docks weren't far, we'd have time after to go to lunch.

"I'll be back," I called to Jack.

"I'll be here," Jack called. He missed seeing Ian standing next to me mouthing the words, "I'll be back" and attempting to look tough. Attempting being the key word. Ian is much more a blonde David Tennant than Arnold Schwarzenegger.

The fog had cooled the air further and I was thankful for the jacket. Dragon-flies flew around us in a rainbow of colors making the air smell like clover. The scent seemed to come from the tiny plumes of flame they spit periodically. Their tiny wings made a low hum as they flitted around us, a nice counterpoint to the sounds of water splashing against the sand.

Ian headed down the hill to the dock. Our dock was not exactly something to write home about, merely a long wooden jetty that stuck out into the lake. The small gravel parking area could accommodate four cars, not that there were any cars on the island, so perhaps it was generously sized.

I passed the clothing store and noticed David, the proprietor, looking out the window. He frowned as he watched us walk by, Ian in front and me trailing slightly behind. Ian was normally one to stand with someone talking, his hands moving as fast as his tongue and probably expressing even more. The fact that he was practically racing down the hill and not waiting for me spoke volumes.

My anxiety ratcheted up, my heart beating faster than it should have for the distance we were going. I may be fat, but I can run when I want to and I'm in decent shape. The movement wasn't raising my heart rate. Worry was. Despite the chill, I felt a cool sweat breaking out. My arms tingled, as they always did when magic was being done.

We got to the dock as the ferry was leaving. Someone was lying on the wooden slats, face up to the fog, which seemed weird.

Ahead of me, Ian stopped.

"We need to go get Xavier," he whispered.

"And why is that?" Bernice asked. She'd come up behind me, silent as ever. The way she walked, she'd probably thought we were strolling along.

"I'm not sure that person's alive," Ian said. "I get nothing from them."

Bernice didn't even raise one of her thin eyebrows before she pulled out her phone and called the police while we all stood at the foot of the dock. When she hung up, she gave us a hard stare.

"I guess I'm the one who gets to go see who it is and if they're alive, Ian's magical sense notwithstanding." She walked, her back straight as a Marine's, as always, her dyed white hair trimmed close about her head, a fine contrast to her dark skin.

I was more than happy to wait there. Being an accountant does not prepare one for seeing dead bodies, and I had yet to see any movement from the person on the dock. At least I hadn't yet seen a ghost.

Chapter Two

The fog lifted quickly, as it always did once the ferry was heading back to either Michigan or Wisconsin. The fog wouldn't be completely gone until the boat was too far for any normal human eye to see. Any mages on board would know the island was there, though we couldn't see it either. I'd looked when I'd gone to my sister's for the holidays.

I heard the sound of golf carts driving down the road. Xavier, the chief of police stepped from the first cart. A thin man of average height with very black skin and hair shorn quite short around his head, he didn't seem like a powerful man, physically, but there was a presence about him that made you take notice.

He glanced at me and Ian, standing in the parking lot, arms crossed, before hurrying down the wooden dock. His feet thudded against the boards and the dock shivered with his steps. In a normal place, I'd worry that he was going to fall over into the water, but here, the island wouldn't let that happen, or perhaps it would. It would just make sure he didn't die.

A second golf cart pulled up, this one pulling a trailer

with all sorts of paraphernalia to move an injured person and probably to examine a dead body at a crime scene. Xavier's deputy, Carl, manned that cart. He stood a few inches over six feet, with fair skin that he claimed never tanned, only freckled. I'd always felt his presence as solid and dependable.

He was one of the few men on the island who was larger than me. I'm not particularly tall, but I am wide. We'd gone out a few times, the interest stronger on Carl's part than mine. I just didn't feel it. Gerald, Carl's former boyfriend, still had feelings. The glares I got whenever I went to Derry's and Gerald was working had made me more than a little uncomfortable. It would take a far stronger interest than I had in Carl to make me put up with that. Fortunately, Carl accepted my feelings with good grace and we remained friendly, if not particularly close.

Carl got out of the golf cart and paused to talk to Bernice who was standing closer to the dock than either Ian or me. A gust of wind blew through carrying their words away from my ears so I couldn't overhear what they were saying. I watched as Bernice gave a single nod and turned away. Carl turned to follow Xavier.

Xavier bent down near the body. Xavier's arm, which at that angle looked a bit too long for his body, reached out and felt for a pulse at the neck. The angle of his head, the stillness of his body against the slight shimmy of the dock spoke to the intensity of his concentration upon the body that lay there.

Xavier stood up and motioned for Carl. The two conferred for a moment. Carl turned and headed back towards us. Xavier stood there, silent, his hands bunched into slight fists. I felt the slightest tingle on my arms when Xavier began to weave magic. Considering the distance, it suggested a spell with a lot of power.

"Wow," Ian muttered.

"The magic?" I said.

He nodded. "I can feel it from here. Hell, it feels like you're doing it."

It made me wonder if that was an effect of the dragon-flies, and only then did I realize that they hadn't followed us into the parking lot. Or if they had, they'd left not long after.

"Did you notice there are no dragon-flies around?" I asked, turning to search for the tiny creatures that had flittered around us as we'd walked to the dock.

Ian looked around, too. "Odd. I've walked down here and along the beach and they've always followed me."

I wondered if the dragon-flies didn't like dead bodies. Or maybe they hadn't liked the fog, or the magic that brought the fog, and had fled until it lifted.

"Well?" Bernice asked when Carl neared. No breeze blew her voice away from us this time.

"Xavier says it looks like Alexander Milton from Far Haven, Maine," Carl said. "But why he was coming here, we don't know."

A chill went down my back. Alexander Milton had been part of the investigative team looking into Damien Bain's many crimes. Far Haven, where Damien was being held, was considered the Alcatraz of magical prisons and as soon as Jewel Island had testified as to what he'd done—via Bernice, of course, the island couldn't actually speak, at least not that I knew of—Damien had been placed in a cell that cut him off from any magic, not that he'd actually had any. What he'd had, he'd stolen from others.

Now, one of the investigators who had questioned us and examined how Damien had subverted the island's magic, was dead. Here.

"How can a dead person take the ferry?" I asked.

"Or at least get off the ferry," Ian said, raising an eyebrow and looking at Carl.

"That's a very good question," Carl said. "I know that in the island's history there have been times when people tried to make it back here to get some magical healing, hoping to survive something that should kill them, but died before arriving. They end up going to the mainland rather than stopping here, unless there was another mage with them."

"I'd have known someone was coming, though. Besides, only one person got off the ferry," Ian said. "Unless the dragon-flies have messed with my magic."

Carl gave Ian a look like he didn't believe they could do that, though why he'd think Ian would be different than the rest of us, I didn't know.

"Bernice didn't say she felt a second person, either," Carl said. "I'd think that if it were a dragon-fly issue that one of you would have felt another person arriving."

I shuddered a little, worried that perhaps Damien had managed to escape, perhaps come back here to finish the job of killing me.

Carl noticed and glanced at me with a slight frown.

"We would have heard if Damien escaped from Far Haven," Ian said, in something approximating a snap. Ian was like that. Sometimes it seemed like he could read my mind. Actually, I felt that a lot on the island, though everyone said they weren't telepathic.

"Damien," Carl said. "While not many people stood by him after he was taken away, a few people…"

He didn't have to name them. Darla had stuck around, even after being let go from the B&B. She'd been Damien's biggest supporter and had blamed me for everything he did, though I'd only been on the island a short time. She'd somehow twisted the story to be that I had forced Damien to murder people so that I could come into my power or something, even though magic didn't work like that.

She'd been unable to find work on the island and had finally left Jewel without so much as a farewell. Not that anyone was really going to miss her. Not after she'd spread all those conspiracy theories.

"Darla?" I whispered.

"I'd have felt her," Ian said.

"Are you sure?" I asked.

Ian nodded.

Darla had been loyal to Damien because he'd been the one to train her magical ability to see ghosts. It was one type of magic Bernice had never been able to master. Despite her training and ability, Darla had hated seeing ghosts. I wondered if she still did.

Darla had been Ian's employee. He'd been the one to fire her when she insisted on Damien's innocence, despite the fact that her boss had nearly been murdered by him along with me. If anyone would have felt Darla's presence on the island, it was Ian—and not just because of the bond he had with the B&B that let him know when someone arrived on the island.

"There's nothing on him to suggest how he died. Xavier is working on figuring it out. I doubt Darla has that kind of power. If she did, I'm not sure she would have let you live." Carl glanced at me, although he could have been talking about either me or Ian.

"She could have learned," I said. I didn't know where she'd gone, but if she'd joined another enclave, she could have been taught how to do other magic. Especially if she went to Far Haven.

"Far Haven wouldn't have her," Ian said quietly, picking up what I was thinking. "The U Council knew about her loyalty to Damien. I reported her harassment of you, as well. They wouldn't have let her go there."

The repeat of his words sounded as if Ian was trying to convince himself as much as me. Perhaps the U Council, shorthand for Union of Enclaves Council, a sort of world-wide government for those who had magic, wasn't as powerful as everyone liked to think.

"That doesn't mean she couldn't have learned something elsewhere," I whispered.

"We don't teach magic that kills," Carl said. "We're not even supposed to have such magic, although in the mundane world, it could probably be done, somehow. I'm thinking something like poison. Maybe taking effect just as he got here. Maybe he was trying to get here and almost made it."

"He'd have had to have fallen off the ferry, then," Ian said. "And if he'd still been intending to come here, even if he were dying, I would have known."

I didn't want to remind him about the dragon-flies interfering with magic or making it go wonky. Maybe he'd feel someone on the island an hour from now instead. I'd had tingling when there wasn't anyone around doing magic, but I'd missed it when Jack did magic to rewarm his coffee an hour earlier.

Bernice continued to stand on the edge of the dock waiting for Xavier. She didn't turn when Carl got a wheeled stretcher out of the trailer. It clanked and clanged as he pushed it over the gravel that made up the little parking area and then quieted when he reached the smoother wood of the dock.

"I don't like this," Ian said. "I feel like someone is coming, someone I don't like. It's hard to explain."

"Like a premonition?" I asked.

"More than that. It's like I know I'm going to have a

visitor at the B&B and I'm not going to like it," he said. "I always know when I'm going to get a visitor or when someone turns up on the island unexpectedly. I tend to have a sense of when someone new to magic is going to be drawn to us, too. It's part of my bond with the building."

I'd talked to Ian about his bond with the B&B before. It seemed strange to me, but he called the place his lover. I wondered if that was why he remained single. As outgoing and fun-loving as Ian was, I couldn't imagine that he wouldn't have been in a relationship if he wanted to be. However, as open as he was about things, there were certain areas of his life that were off-limits. Relationships were one of them.

We stood there, the cool breeze beating against us now and again, waves crashing mournfully against the island. The sky darkened with ominous gray clouds. A storm was coming. I suspected it wasn't just going to be a rain storm, either.

Chapter Three

Waiting on Carl and Xavier to move the body meant that it was late before Ian and I could even think about lunch, though with the timing, I had a feeling thinking about it was all we'd end up doing. Sadly, that was a state I was altogether too familiar with considering we weren't far beyond tax time.

Thick drops of rain had started to fall by the time we left the parking area. As soon as we stepped away from the gravel covered square, the dragon-flies encircled us, buzzing around us.

Bernice passed us heading up the hill, lost in her own thoughts, back ramrod straight. She'd given us a half-wave as she passed, which was downright friendly for her. Normally it's hard to tell if she's even noticed you exist unless she's offering you some level of criticism.

Ian walked more slowly with his trademark sashay, no longer in a hurry to find out what was going on at the dock, though he did walk a bit faster, perhaps hoping to beat the worst of the rain.

"We can skip lunch if you want," I said. We both

needed to get back to work. I could put off a few things or hand off a few tasks to Jack, but since Darla had left, Ian only had Edie's part-time help, and she was rather slow.

"I don't really want," Ian said, "but we probably should. I have ordering to do. And maybe back at the B&B I can put my finger on the feeling that someone is coming. Being inside helps."

I nodded my head as if I understood, though I didn't, not really. I'd gotten somewhat used to not understanding things on Jewel, so I didn't let it bother me too much.

We didn't talk much as we walked up the hill. It wasn't the incline so much as the fact that we were each lost in our own thoughts about what the body meant. I worried that somehow someone linked to Damien had snuck onto the island and wanted to kill me. I was probably being paranoid, but while people had periodically not liked me, as is true with most people, no one had ever wanted to kill me before I'd arrived on Jewel.

I reminded myself I was bonded to the island now which would make killing me more difficult. But I could be killed on the ferry, and who knew if the island could be subverted, particularly when the dragon-flies were around. Damien, after all, wasn't supposed to have been able to do what he did.

The accounting office waited for me. I paused and watched Ian jog up to the B&B as the rain started coming down harder. I huddled under the porch by our door making sure he got to where he was going. I didn't know exactly why I felt worried for him.

Meanwhile, four dragon-flies hovered with me. Two seemed to fly at me and then off as if insisting I go inside, rather like someone making a shoo hand movement. When I finally did, one breathed out a thread of fire at me, almost like a sigh, before disappearing over my head, leaving me with the faint scent of clover.

I wish I understood the creatures and how they worked. I mean, the shoo movement could have been taken as a warning to get inside before the rain or before something else happened. It could also be just an action that they randomly took from time to time. No one on the island really seemed to understand them and most people were just fine with that.

The one person who wouldn't be okay with not understanding them was Lauren, our head librarian. I resolved that after I did some work this afternoon, I'd go talk to her.

"I heard there was a body at the dock," Jack said coming out of his office.

Of course he had. I mean, Jewel was small. Everyone had probably heard, though I didn't know how because Ian and I weren't talking and I couldn't imagine Bernice gossiping, nor Xavier or Carl even if they'd had the time.

I frowned.

"Pegs was at the grocery store and saw the golf cart pulling away with what looked like a body. As they weren't in a hurry, she figured the person was dead," Jack explained before I could even ask.

"There was. I think it looked like Alexander Milton from Far Haven," I said.

"Really? Who brought him?" Jack asked.

"No one we can find."

"But…" Jack was at a loss for words. Then he straightened and said, "But Ian's the Innkeeper. The Innkeeper always knows. And so does the Teacher and the Mayor."

"The Innkeeper?" I asked. Ian was the proprietor of the B&B, which was pretty much the only place to stay on the island unless you stayed with friends. As the building grows to expand to hold as many people as it needed, it wasn't a problem, not that we got that many visitors on Jewel.

"It's his magic," Jack said. "Whoever bonds with the B&B or Inn or Hotel or whatever the enclave has, becomes the Innkeeper. It's why his magic works differently than ours. He's linked to the building which is linked directly to the island. It was that link that allowed him to see through the illusions that Damien gave all of us and was able to rescue you. Buildings can't be fooled, not like that. Any magic he does when he consciously links to the building using some of its power won't be affected by the dragonflies, either."

"And his title is Innkeeper?" I asked.

Jack nodded. "There are rumors he has more powers but no one has really dared ask. You know how Ian is. He'll entertain you with stories for hours, laugh at himself, laugh at everyone in such a way that no one gets mad, but you never really talk to him about important stuff."

Jack was right, which surprised me. First, because I hadn't noticed that. I mean I knew better than to ask Ian about a relationship but never considered asking him more about his magic. He'd seemed rather forthcoming to me about it because I'd been new and he'd been explaining basic things. The other surprising thing was that Jack was so perceptive. He was always so worried about things and making sure we all had enough of whatever we might need that it didn't seem like he'd have time to read people.

"You're right," I said. "I always felt like I knew Ian but…"

"He's like that with everyone. I mean, I know you know he's gay and all so I didn't worry about you hoping for more than friendship. Lauren had her sights set on him at first, but now she knows better. I think Ian felt badly that it didn't work but he said he just wasn't ready. It might be that the B&B takes all his energy and there's no room for a relationship or maybe he's just got some romantic notion that there's a guy who hasn't come into his magic yet that's going to show up here and sweep him off his feet."

"Lauren's a woman," I said. "I'd have thought she'd know better. It's not like Ian hides his sexuality."

"Well…" Jack started and stopped. "Maybe she didn't think everyone thought of her as a woman."

"Huh?" I felt very dim. Lauren was a nicely dressed woman. Her outfits were a little on the retro side, particularly the way she wore her scarves, but no one would ever take her for a man.

"She's…" once again Jack trailed off.

I waited. This was awkward. Finally, it hit me. I'd never even considered that perhaps the gender assigned Lauren at birth didn't match who she actually was.

Jack once again surprised me by being more perceptive than I was. I really needed to start paying better attention to people.

The silence lengthened and Jack still seemed as if he was struggling to say something that would get the point across without being offensive. I didn't think it was my place to go around gossiping about Lauren. If she wanted me to know more, she'd tell me. Instead, I changed the subject back to Ian.

"I'm glad you were willing to look out for me and any potential romantic intrigue," I finally said after that rather lengthy silence. I still felt rather like a peeping tom and hoped that Jack would take the hint to talk about something else.

The whole discussion made me uncomfortable and I didn't want to bring that discomfort into the library and maybe act in a way that made Lauren uncomfortable, so I decided I'd put off going to the library that afternoon.

Perhaps I'd stop by the next day to ask her about dragon-flies. I could go at lunch and get answers rather than feeling like I was playing hooky.

I headed back to my office to get to work. After all, that's what I was paid for. I was almost there when the front door banged open.

I jumped and looked back. Darla stood there, looking furious. Apparently, she was the person that Ian had almost been sensing, though he would be mortified to know he'd somehow missed her, of all people.

Chapter Four

Darla had been one of the youngest people on the island, barely younger than Ian. Though he acted like a teenager, the lines on his face showed that he wasn't as young as he might be taken for. Darla, however, was fresh-faced and wide-eyed. Although, now, her eyes were a little less wide and the look on her face was anything but fresh.

She'd cut her long red hair short so she no longer wore the single braid down her back. Now her hair framed her face and had a slight curl on one side but not the other. Her jeans were worn and her jacket looked crumpled, as if she'd slept in it. Both were wet from the rain.

The dragon-flies were buzzing around, loudly. A few were spitting threads of fire out, like tiny creatures sticking their tongues at her. For the first time that I'd seen, several came into the building. Darla swatted at them.

"What the hell did you do?" she demanded.

I looked around, wondering what she was talking about. I hadn't done anything and if she was referring to anything that happened with Damien, she knew those facts well. Jack stood frozen by the door to his office, mouth slightly open.

"You." Darla snapped, pointing at me. The dragon-flies were more agitated.

"I don't know what you're talking about," I said.

"You got me kicked out of Hidden Rock," she snapped.

"I did nothing," I repeated. "I didn't even know where you were, much less where Hidden Rock is. Is it an enclave?" I asked.

"You know damned well it is! You're the one who called them and told them I loved Damien and couldn't be trusted," Darla snapped.

I shook my head. "I did no such thing."

"Three weeks ago, I was fired from my job at a café there because they said Holly Baxter called and told them I had participated in some questionable magical practices. Two weeks ago, I was kicked out of the enclave," Darla snapped, glaring at me.

"It wasn't me," I said.

"Three weeks ago we were at the tail end of taxes," Jack added. He normally didn't engage in confrontations. Once again he surprised me standing up to Darla and even glaring at her. Maybe it was the dragon-flies. Maybe they made us act strangely, too.

"So?" Darla asked.

"Like we weren't swamped? As if Holly would have had time to call anyone?" Jack said. He shook his head and darted away, into his office. I hoped that he called someone for help while he hid away in his office.

That left Darla to glare at me, the dragon-flies still fluttering around her head.

"You found time, though, didn't you?" Darla snapped.

"I didn't call," I said. "I had no idea where you were. I was just glad I didn't have to deal with you here."

That sort of deflated her somewhat, as if she hadn't even thought that getting her fired would bring her back to the island.

"How exactly did you get here without Ian noticing?" I asked. "We were all down at the dock and there was a dead man there."

Darla frowned.

"Maybe you need to talk to Xavier." I tried to be gentle as I said it, but of course that didn't work.

Darla swore some more as she turned and left the office, hurrying out into the rain. Most of the dragon-flies gave chase, following behind, but a couple, two red and one a bright purple stayed behind and fluttered around the door. The purple one puffed circles of smoke the size of my pinkie finger. The smoke seemed to swallow its head every time it flew through one.

I felt a faint tingle of magic across my arms. I wondered who was doing a spell but there was only Jack in the other room. I heard him talking on the phone, so he had called someone. He couldn't be doing magic. Darla was already far enough away that her magic shouldn't cause any problems.

At least I thought so until a heavy gust of wind blasted in through the door and knocked me on my butt. If I were Jack's size I'd probably have been thrown back into the conversation pit of the room, maybe even hit the windows.

The dragon-flies who had stayed gave little twitters like squirrels chittering at each other and then flew out the door, which closed after them, leaving me gaping at it, wondering what had happened.

Chapter Five

I'd picked myself up by the time Jack finished on the phone and hurried out. His hair wasn't its usual tidy self. He'd clearly run his fingers through it. He bit his lower lip with his upper teeth as he practically ran out of the office and stared at me.

"What happened?" he asked.

"A gust of wind hit me. A powerful one. It had to have been magic, but Darla was running down the street." Then I remembered that sometimes magic got delayed with the dragon-flies.

"She doesn't have air magic, not enough to do that," Jack said quietly. "Ghosts were her thing, though she hated it. That's why she was so close to Damien."

"Well, someone did it," I said. "I felt magic tingling down my arms and the wind came."

"Even the dragon-fly weirdness doesn't exactly explain Darla being able to do that. Someone else had to have been out there," Jack said. "I called the police station. Rose will send someone."

Rose was the receptionist. She was an old woman with

a head shake that reminded me of a bobble-head doll. As slow as she moved, I'd be able to walk to the station and tell Xavier what happened myself before she made it across the room to tell him. Still, this wasn't an emergency and maybe, if Rose was fast, Xavier would get out of the station in time to run into Darla.

"Thanks," I said. "Did you know where Darla was?"

Jack shook his head. "I'd heard a couple of rumors that she'd found a job in another enclave but didn't know which one. It couldn't have been Far Haven because they wouldn't have let her be that close to Damien. She'd been too much under his spell. Looks like she still might be."

Maybe that was why she'd accused me of calling. Or perhaps someone else had called and claimed to be me. I didn't know who would do that to either me or to Darla but I couldn't rule it out.

"I wonder why she came back. I mean, yes, she said I called and got her fired, but even if someone impersonated me and that happened, why come here?" I asked, looking at Jack.

Jack's eyes widened a bit and he looked uncomfortable. Finally, after much hemming and hawing, "I don't know."

Neither did I. I also worried about the fact that Ian hadn't known that Darla was on the island. I pulled out my phone and called over to the B&B.

"Miss me already darling?" Ian's voice was light, though I thought I detected a hint of tension.

"Darla was just here," I told him. "She came in on the ferry."

"So that's who it was. The B&B knew someone was here but not who it was. I bet Darla's had some things change in her life. She was so familiar to the building, having worked here for months, it wouldn't recognize her if she'd changed a lot. And I mean, let's be real, after she sided with Damien she was not the same person," Ian said. "Still, how did she hide?"

"I don't know," I said. "She came in here and accused me of getting her fired."

"Did you?" Ian asked.

"No. I didn't even know where she was." I mean, Ian wouldn't judge me if I'd done something like that, but I had hoped he knew me well enough to know I wouldn't be so vindictive. I'd just been glad she wasn't on the island. She'd made me uncomfortable with her glares and her innuendos.

"I don't think anyone knew where she was, although if you did know and didn't tell me, I'd have been annoyed," Ian said. "But, if no one here knew where she was, she had to have been lying, or else someone lied to her about why they let her go."

"Could someone here have pretended to be me?" I asked.

"If I didn't know where she was, then it was the best kept secret on the island," Ian said. "Which means I doubt anyone here knew. I suppose someone could have randomly called every enclave restaurant in the United States and asked for Darla but that would be a hella lot a work for very little reward…"

Ian's voice trailed off.

"What?"

"What if they wanted her to come back?" Ian said. "What if someone is pushing her to come back here for some reason? Let's be real. Darla might have changed enough that the B&B didn't recognize her, but I had a feeling *someone* was around. I just couldn't be certain. I should have been certain there was another person here. Especially inside the building. Something else is going on, like maybe high-powered magic, enough to mess with the B&B and that's like messing with the island."

Knots formed in my stomach. I'd just relaxed from the busiest time of year and now I was stressing out again. I didn't like this at all. I wanted to know exactly what was going on with Darla.

"I have to go," I told Ian when I saw Xavier slip through the door.

Chapter Six

Xavier wore gray slacks and a navy rain jacket that dripped water on the floor. He spent a moment hanging his head outside shaking off the water from his close cropped hair. Then he turned to me, his sharp brown eyes taking in everything, from where I stood to the way the raindrops splashed against the windows behind me.

"You said Darla was here?" he asked.

"She left a little bit ago. Jack had probably barely hung up with Rose when she left," I said. "She was pretty angry with me."

"Why?" Xavier asked. He pulled a small notebook from a pocket beneath the jacket. The pen he pulled out was a shiny deep purple and looked more feminine that I would have expected from the chief of police.

I explained that Darla thought I had called and gotten her fired from her job at Hidden Rock.

"Did you know she was there?" Xavier asked.

I shook my head but said nothing more.

"I hadn't heard where she'd gone. For some reason, I thought she'd stayed close, maybe worked in the mundane world or worked her way towards Maine to be closer to Far Haven." Xavier was clearly thinking out loud.

I'd have expected the same thing as Xavier, and it wasn't lost on me that he was almost parroting exactly what my thoughts had been. I wondered if there was some strange dragon-fly magic at work or maybe we'd been led to believe that was where she was.

I suggested the last part. If we were being influenced again, we needed to know.

Xavier wrote that down, then had a look at Jack.

Jack shrugged. "I figured she was out looking for a job. I hadn't thought about Maine, but yeah, I never thought of her as going to another enclave. I guess it was more because it seemed like it would be easier for her to coast in the ordinary world."

Once again Jack put his finger on something that I had sort of known but hadn't paid attention to. I shuddered to think what other things about me he might have noticed over these months as we worked together on taxes, me doing the more involved stuff, him doing the simpler ones that I checked over and signed off on.

I told Xavier about the phone call with Ian explaining that Ian hadn't known Darla was there, but sort of knew there was someone else on the island, just not who or where.

"So he was aware of someone, but not who they were or what they needed?" Xavier clarified.

"That was what I understood, but you'd need to ask him directly. He thought that maybe Darla had changed enough that the B&B didn't recognize her, so couldn't tell him who she was," I added.

Xavier raised an eyebrow and made a note of that.

"Did she threaten to hurt you?"

I thought back but realized that she'd just barged in

like a tank and started yelling. I said as much. I also said that she ran out and after that a huge gust of wind had knocked me down.

"You don't have a lot of air magic, right?" Xavier asked.

I wondered what it was like to be a police officer some place like Jewel where knowing what sort of magic each person possessed had a bearing on the crime. Of course, generally speaking Jewel was a pretty quiet island. Xavier mostly taught self-defense and made sure no one was littering and occasionally helped out someone who'd had too much to drink. I heard that he'd arrested a mage or two who had come to Jewel to try and hide out from ordinary police for crimes they'd committed in that world. So long as they hadn't used magic, he'd turn them over with a spell to keep them from using magic against law enforcement.

"Air is probably my weakest element," I said.

"Darla didn't have air magic either," Jack said quietly.

Xavier looked up at him. Jack looked down at his feet and everywhere but at the chief.

"Thanks for that. Did you see which way she went?"

I shook my head.

"No, but Ian said something that seemed important when I talked to him on the phone," I said.

Xavier waited.

I explained about Ian's suggestion that someone might be pushing Darla to come here.

"I mean, why come here if she thought I had her fired? If someone called and had me fired, they'd be the last person I wanted to see." Case in point. My ex-husband's family had owned the company where I worked and he'd suggested it would be best if I left. He was definitely the last person I wanted to see, although there might have been some other emotional issues there as well.

"Call if she comes back, especially if she threatens you. The island won't like it and dragon-flies or not, it won't let you get hurt, not now. I'd say you're in less danger than anyone else considering that you saved the enclave from being a slave to Damien," Xavier said.

I couldn't say I felt that safe but overall, I did feel relatively protected on Jewel Island. An umbrella stand appeared but Xavier ignored it, preferring to run out to the golf cart parked out front. The rain still lashed down so hard I thought I understood what it felt like to be a fish.

Xavier had leaped into the cart before I even shut the door. I admit to being a bit slow in my movements, but even so, the Chief of Police was fast. Faster than Darla had seemed, though she'd run as if her life depended upon it. Maybe it did. If someone had been pushing her to come to Jewel Island, maybe there was something here that could hurt her. Especially if the island didn't recognize her.

It was almost enough to make me go out and try and flag down Xavier to mention that. But the rain still pounded on the roof and he'd been pulling the little golf cart out onto the road even as I'd closed the door. I'd never make it. Better to call him. Perhaps in a little bit. I wasn't particularly thrilled about talking to Rose.

Jack had gone back to hide in his office. He'd probably been more social that afternoon than he normally was in a week and had to work off that anxiety. I said nothing as I moved back to my office, still thinking about how surprisingly perceptive he was.

I walked into my office only to find the window covered with dragon-flies. The window is huge, starting about a foot off the floor and going up to the ceiling. It took up the entire ten foot width of the wall, though there were narrow columns in between to hold the glass in place.

Dragon-flies covered that whole area. I'd never seen so many in one place, despite their propensity to flitter around the heads of various people or to follow them around. I stepped back out and looked at the main window, but I hadn't managed to miss seeing them holding onto the glass in the main room. They were just staring into my office.

Their eyes were just large enough that when I got close, I knew they were looking at me. Heads turned and watched as I got near the window. Not a single one blew threads of fire or hissed out puffs of smoke from their tiny nostrils. They just watched.

A single orange dragon-fly left the window and a green one took its place, as if they were creating a protective net around the glass. A huge gust of wind blew off the lake. I peered between the tiny dragon-flies and saw a large wave crash against the cliff, white foam leaping over the side and reaching up to hit the building. The crash was large enough to shake the office.

I'd not experience that before.

I looked up at the dark clouds in time to see a funnel forming, like a giant maw in the sky.

"Jack, get down, away from the windows!" I shouted, even as I followed my own advice and ran for the supply room, which was probably the safest place. There weren't any windows there and it was on the other side of the building from where the funnel was building.

Jack scurried into the room with me, closing the door and hunching down behind the work island that sat in the middle of the room.

"I've never seen anything like that over the lake. I didn't know Jewel would allow such a thing."

I heard the wind crash against the building. Felt the shaking. I heard a sound like a train racing by, but without the helpful shriek of a horn.

Then it was gone. No sound of glass breaking. No sound of the train leaving. Everything was just silent.

"Is this the calm in the middle?" Jack asked as if he believed we'd been lifted off to Oz.

I shrugged. I had only slight knowledge of how tornados worked. By and large I'd lived too far north to have to worry about them.

We both waited until my legs started to cramp. When I stood up, Jack followed. Even if we'd had a silent moment in the eye of a storm, though I thought that was for hurricanes not tornados, it had gone on longer than it needed to.

Stepping into my office, I noticed that the dragon-flies were gone from the glass, but they continued to flit around outside. It was almost as if they'd been guarding my window from the funnel cloud.

I tossed that idea aside. The island would have protected me, or should have. But the dragon-flies seemed to have stepped up to stand guard. I had no idea why or how. Something was going on and it appeared that, once again, I was involved in things I didn't understand.

Chapter Seven

Ordinary rain continued throughout the afternoon without any new funnel clouds. Oddly, no one else seemed to have experienced the tornado. I called Ian, but he'd heard only that a few people thought they saw a water spout, not an actual tornado. I would have written the experience off as my overactive imagination except that Jack was there and so were the dragon-flies.

I walked home in the rain, safely dry beneath one of Jewel's magical umbrellas. When it began to rain urns appeared by any doors, whether it was a house or the office or perhaps Derry's restaurant, holding umbrellas. I thought they held maybe three umbrellas, but the urns never ran out no matter how many people might need to grab one.

The best part, though, was that each umbrella kept you dry, not just when rain fell without wind but from rain that might be blowing towards you. I sometimes felt like I was inside my own little protected capsule. Only my feet ever got wet and that had more to do with the puddles and rivulets that formed on the walking paths. Really, though, I would have thought the island could have fixed that, too, but for whatever reason it had chosen not to.

If I ever moved away from Jewel Island, I would miss the umbrella magic the most—assuming, of course that I could still see the friends I had made. Heck, when I went to my sister's at Christmas, I had missed having a magical umbrella when it sleeted.

While I loved fitting into seats and being able to buy clothing that I liked and know that David could make it fit me, those things were simply nice perks, but the umbrellas...well, those were something else.

My home on the island was a single-level condominium just over the hill from where I worked, a five-minute walk if I hurried, ten if I tarried to look out at the lake or if I were walking carefully due to snow or ice. It was the place that had chosen me, according to the real estate agent, but I still felt as if I'd made the decision. The condominium had been perfect. Of course, the island probably knew exactly what I wanted even if I didn't have an image of the perfect home in my mind.

I went home and was greeted by the two cats. Peony, a lovely calico had adopted me just days after I'd arrived on the island. Tulip, a beautiful Siamese, adopted me shortly after I'd found my house. The two got along well and while they were magic, they certainly acted like ordinary cats when it came to getting fed.

After dinner, for both me and the cats, I felt at loose ends. Normally, on a rainy evening, I'd have watched some television. But that evening I couldn't settle. I did a load of laundry, though there was less in there than normal. I cleaned a few things that didn't really need cleaning, but made the place smell of pine cleaner and lemon.

Outside, the clouds hung so low that instead of evening light, it was black as night. And it was still raining. Perhaps not as hard as earlier, but hard enough to keep me from walking outside or even walking to the clubhouse to work out in the gym. Part of me considered doing so anyway. The umbrellas would make it easy but I couldn't settle even long enough to make a decision.

I sat down for a minute, channel surfing, hoping for something to take my mind off of things. Peony jumped up next to me and rubbed her orange, black, and white head against my arm. She gave a little merp and then started to purr, staring at me with her large yellow eyes.

My arms tingled. Calm settled over me. I realized she'd done a calming spell.

Not feeling so much anxious energy, I was able to sit for a moment and gather my thoughts, and come up with an idea of what I really wanted to do. I stood up, annoying Peony, who leaped from the sofa and went to find Tulip, who was probably already settled on my bed.

I headed to my secondary bedroom which served as both a home office and a makeshift guest room should one of my sisters or their kids come to visit.

I took my laptop from the white Ikea desk and settled on the daybed sofa. Plumping the green and blue pillows just so, I sat in a half-lotus position to do some searching. I put in Darla's name. Unfortunately, with a last name like Edwards, her name was all too common and I had to spend some time thinking about ways to narrow my search.

Having learned that Hidden Rock was in Arizona, I limited the search to news about Darla Edwards in Arizona. This narrowed down the hits to a more manageable number, or at least not such a ridiculous number. The first four links were obituaries for two different women with the same name. They'd both died within the last ten years. Another was for a woman retiring—not one of the Darlas who had died. Another article talked about a young woman who was selling handcrafted beaded purses.

That didn't sound like the Darla I knew, but perhaps she'd changed. I finally came across a link that might have been the correct Darla Edwards. A young woman reported a break in at the hotel where she was staying in Tucson. As I wasn't familiar with exactly where in Arizona Hidden Rock was, I didn't know if Tucson was nearby. Even if it wasn't, perhaps it had happened as Darla had traveled there slowly. I mean, it was a main city.

The police could find no evidence of a break-in except for a slightly damaged door and the word of the woman named Darla Edwards. It appeared nothing had been done and I could find no further information on the incident.

I bit my lip as I thought. Maybe Darla was the one in danger. Maybe her anger at me was really fear. But it didn't make sense for someone to want her to come here, unless the person who wanted to harm her was already on the island.

Of course, even having changed so much that the B&B didn't recognize her, Darla would soon bond with the island. If someone wanted to hurt her, they would need to do so before she was noticed.

Nothing was making sense. I tried on other ideas. Perhaps Darla hadn't wanted Ian to know she was here and was purposely hiding herself. I didn't know if that was possible, but from what I'd learned if someone wanted something badly enough, magic usually found a way. I had to admit that from what I knew, Darla didn't seem to have that much power, but perhaps someone had helped her, though I couldn't figure out why she wouldn't want Ian to know she was back. She couldn't possibly suspect that Ian wanted to hurt her, at least I didn't think so.

I sighed, trying to put the pieces together. I hadn't found any answers. Just more questions.

Chapter Eight

The next morning was the weekly Eggs Benedict breakfast at the B&B. The dining room would be crowded, but from my perspective, along with most of the other residents, it was totally worth it. The Eggs Benedict was amazing. I hurried through my morning routine, making sure the cats had plenty of food, not that they would let me forget.

Then, I headed out, with plenty of time to eat. The morning had dawned bright and sunny, though the pavement was still wet from the rain the night before.

The day had the fresh after-rain smell that I loved and the sun warmed my shoulders. I wasn't as relaxed and calm as I had been after Peony had put the spell on me but I wasn't as stressed as I might have been. The night before I had spent plenty of time trying to figure out who might want to hurt Darla and why they wanted her here, but I hadn't come up with any ideas, particularly not one that also answered why Alexander Milton, from Far Haven, had been found dead on the island's dock.

Dragon-flies buzzed around, flitting and circling before

flying off to land around the flowers. Waves lapped against the shore more gentle in their caress than the day before. In the distance I heard one of the golf cart engines start up.

The police weren't the only ones with golf carts. There was one at the medical center and several residents had their own. Bernice told me a lot of the residents preferred those over scooters because it was easier to have a second person ride with them. I figured it was nice to have a cover rather than the open air riding of a scooter, too, particularly in bad weather. So far, I'd resisted getting one. I liked walking and there was just enough personal insecurity about what people would think of a fat woman using a golf cart when she could walk that it hadn't made the investment worth it.

Gretchen walked into the B&B garden just as I got to the fence. She lived further inland where she grew herbs that she delivered to the restaurants. She also had plenty of medicinal herbs, too, from times when the island had an acupuncturist and before that, a naturopath.

Both practitioners had ended up leaving the island. One had wanted to start a family and the island had no facilities for children. It was the main reason people left. Well, that and the weather. A lot of people retired to an enclave in a warmer area.

"Morning," I said.

"Good morning," Gretchen said. She smiled as she greeted me and her whole face lit up. "Are you joining anyone or would you like to join me? I hate eating alone, but I hate missing out on the eggs."

"I would love to join you," I said.

Gretchen was older than I was and had been around the island quite a bit longer. Since becoming mayor,

Bernice was no longer teaching the new mages. Gretchen had taken on that task. Her general good nature suggested she was a far less trying task master than Bernice, who had insisted upon finishing my training even as the duties of being mayor began to take up more and more of her time.

The dining room was just beginning to get busy. Dirk and Bill, as always in their twin flannel shirts, were already at their table. I'd learned that they farmed goats out towards the far end of the island. They both waved at us, though I knew they were mostly greeting Gretchen. She'd taught them a lot about the plants they could grow for the goats to make their wool softer and to increase their milk production.

Apparently, Bill made soap and Ginny, an older woman who lived on the island, spun yarn. She didn't purchase the wool from them. Instead, she split her profits, which, to my mind wasn't as lucrative, but Ginny said between her pension and social security, she did just fine without any extra income at all.

A few other people were already seated and eating. The round two-top tables and rectangular four-top tables were nearly filled. The room smelled of Canadian bacon and the ever-present coffee. Edie was pouring water and bringing around the coffee pot. She nodded at us.

"I heard Darla dropped by your office yesterday," Gretchen said.

Nodding, I asked, "Did anyone ever find her?"

"I haven't heard of any more sightings. I did hear that Xavier found out that Alexander was supposed to be on vacation in the Caribbean."

"I think he may have made a wrong turn." And not one that would be enjoyable. In May, Lake Michigan was not exactly a body of water you wanted to swim in.

Gretchen generously smiled at my little joke just as Edie came by with coffee for me and a pot of hot water for Gretchen. I watched as Gretchen pulled out her own packet of tea. She had a small light weave muslin bag for steeping. She'd probably made the tea herself. I knew she had some camellias and she probably dried the leaves.

I breathed in the rich scent of the coffee and half closed my eyes.

"I can't imagine what he wanted here," Gretchen said. "The enclave on Far Haven is upset about his death, of course. He was deputy mayor there and lots of people looked up to him. The mayor did the legal stuff and kept in touch with other enclaves. They're far more connected than most because they have the prison there. Alex was the one who talked to the locals and made sure the enclave ran smoothly."

"Who took over when he was on vacation?" I asked, sipping my drink and feeling the warm caffeine waking up my cells.

"They all pitch in. I mean, vacations don't last forever and Far Haven is smaller than most enclaves because you don't just find it. You're sent there, either as a prisoner or because you're needed there in some capacity. Xavier worked there for a few years before coming back here. I guess he hated it so much that they found someone to replace him so he could go elsewhere."

"I did not know that," I said.

Gretchen nodded. "I think the council decided to send him here because of rumors about Damien. Unfortunately, Xavier's magic wasn't strong enough to withstand the illusions that Damien wove and he fell under Damien's spell just like the rest of us. Except you, of course. And Ian, but only because he's connected to the B&B."

Which wasn't unlike what was happening now. We

knew someone had to have come on the island. A thought occurred to me.

"Could another spell have made us all forget what we'd seen?" I asked. "You know, if someone came on the island with Alexander's body?"

"It would take more power than any of us have. Damien was only able to do it because he was drawing power from the island. Besides, you saw Darla and we all remembered that."

Darla wasn't exactly a big woman. Frail almost. While Alexander Milton hadn't appeared to be a particularly large man, a dead body wasn't easy to carry and I couldn't imagine she'd pushed him off the ferry on her own. Besides, after what I'd learned about the break-in at her hotel room, Darla seemed to be running from someone. Or, perhaps, something.

Ian sashayed out with our plates of Eggs Benedict. He served them with Potatoes O'Brien and cups of fruit—real fruit, not the fruit cocktail from a can stuff. Today the fruit included strawberries, raspberries, and sliced kiwi. My mouth watered.

"What do we know about Alexander Milton?" I asked after Ian had made sure everything was okay.

Gretchen finished swallowing her first bite of the eggs. She stabbed one of her potato pieces and swirled it around in the Hollandaise while she chewed and then spoke, almost leaning on her fork as she did so.

"He was the best. Powerful," she said. "It's why he was the one who took Damien to Far Haven. Because even if our spells had failed to hold him, Alexander was one of the few people who could have held him on his own. If Alexander didn't die naturally, and someone carried him off the ferry, then it would have taken several people to murder him, at least with magic."

"I looked Darla up online," I confessed. "There was a police report that I found from Tucson that said someone broke into her hotel room. It made me wonder if someone was out to get her, maybe driving her here for some reason."

Gretchen cocked her head and took another bite. I savored my own eggs, chewing slowly. Perhaps this wasn't a conversation to have while eating such amazing food.

When she'd finished chewing, not eating any faster than I was, Gretchen frowned a bit. "I have no idea why anyone would drive her here. If anything, Jewel is more protected than most places. The island itself now knows what Damien is. It won't be fooled again. The magic is somewhat sentient and it can learn. It might not fully understand people, but there are reasons it protects its own from being harmed on the island. It learned how bad we can be to each other. While Ian says the island doesn't exactly recognize Darla, it will remember her soon enough, probably already does. Of course, I get hints that the island isn't happy, although I'm not certain exactly what that means," Gretchen said.

It didn't occur to me that the island could be happy or unhappy, but that was just another odd thing about enclaves.

"So why drop a dead body here and drive Darla here?" I asked, after finishing a bite of potatoes.

"That's a good question, isn't it?" Gretchen said. "Part of me wants to say that because we're the ones that the magic trusts to figure it out. Maybe there's someone out there with information, but they're terrified and are hoping we step in. But I can't imagine who that would be. It might also mean that Alexander was dead before he got on that ferry, not killed while aboard, like we've been assuming."

"Or maybe there were plenty of mages who had

worked together to kill Alexander while he was on the ferry. Then they dumped him here," Gretchen continued

"Could the number of mages it would've taken to kill Alexander have gotten off the ferry without anyone knowing?" I asked. I'd been there, though. The ferry had hardly started pulling away when I'd stepped into the parking lot. That many people couldn't just disappear, though I suppose invisibility was possible. Ian would have sensed them, at least from what I understood.

Gretchen shook her head. "I expect that Darla got off. Alexander could have been dropped from the deck, I suppose, if there were mages there who had no intention of getting off, but that would have to be a last-minute decision or the ferry wouldn't have stopped here."

"Unless it knew that Darla wanted to get off at the island," I said. "And those people knew it as well."

"It doesn't explain why Ian didn't know about her," Gretchen said. "The island doesn't recognize new people per se, but Ian always knows when someone is here. This time he didn't, not really."

"He said it was because Darla was different or something," I said.

"Once he knew she was here that could explain it, but it wouldn't explain why he didn't sense someone getting off the ferry," Gretchen said. "If he hasn't admitted that, he's scared, and I don't like to think of the sorts of things that can scare the Innkeeper. The stallion may be the heart of the island's magic, but the Innkeeper is the heart of the island's ability to interact with humans."

"But shouldn't Ian have been able to neutralize Damien, then?"

"The Innkeeper doesn't come into his powers fully formed. It's a slow process as Ian bonds ever more closely to the B&B, which is part of the island's magic. He'll live longer than we will because of that. Damien probably would have made sure to set Ian up on a trip off island in the near future, to take care of him. Neither of them would have had their full powers, but Damien's a killer. Ian isn't. He wouldn't be the Innkeeper if he was."

There was always something new to learn. I wondered how much of that Ian knew about himself. It wasn't like he shared that information, yet everyone else seemed so easy with it, though I was still learning. Of course, I was still the newest person on the island.

I think Gretchen, or maybe Jack, had told me there were usually two or three people a year who made it to the island, so any day now I could lose my newcomer status. It would be nice to not be the only one who didn't know things.

We ate our breakfast mostly in companionable silence and when we did talk, the conversation turned to more restful topics than who had murdered a man and left him on the dock. I wasn't a police officer so I doubted I would have to be involved in solving the mystery. I just hoped Darla didn't bring whoever was chasing her to my door.

As we were finishing up, Darla walked into the B&B. She looked around at all of us, giving me a particular glare, though I'm not sure she looked particularly pleased to see anyone.

"Where's Ian?" she demanded.

Ian walked out of the kitchen, with only the slightest hint of a sashay and even that seemed forced. Tension radiated from his body.

Darla brought up a knife and pointed it at him.

Ian stopped.

Darla threw the knife overhand. I heard gasps, one of them coming from me.

The knife, of course, didn't come anywhere close to

hitting Ian. He didn't even bother to put up a hand. He was in the B&B, and I suspected this was his place of power.

Darla made a sound like a growl before turning and running from the room.

Chapter Nine

A couple of people stood up to watch as Darla fled the room. I turned in my seat as she raced out the door, but it's not like I'm particularly fast so I didn't go after her. No one else did either. I didn't know if they didn't think there was any need or if they were all too busy enjoying their breakfasts to get up and leave.

Ian stood there in shock. "What the hell was that?" he asked, though he didn't ask it of anyone in particular.

"A very foolish girl," Bill said from his place at the table. He'd finished his meal and he and Dirk were enjoying their coffee.

"Besides that," Ian said. "Who throws knives at people in my inn? Or anywhere. It's not exactly a great way to assassinate someone even on the mainland. And that was Darla? Of course it was Darla. I know that." He shook his head, clearly rattled.

Gretchen stood up and put a hand on Ian. My arms tingled as she used magic to help him calm down. Ian normally handles a crisis reasonably well. He'd been a rock when Damien and Sharon had tried to kill me. Maybe the difference was that he was the target now.

He held up a hand. "I'm fine. Really."

Gretchen stepped back. The tingling on my arms stopped.

"I don't get why she'd even try that. Or why she'd come here just to throw a knife."

"Anything special about the knife?" I asked. It had fallen to the floor a few feet in front of Ian. The throw had been well-aimed and had good distance. I wondered how many people could actually make that sort of throw even if it didn't hit the target.

I'd gotten a lucky hit on Damien when I'd thrown a knife, though I'd inadvertently had a bit of practice when I'd gone to an axe throwing session with my sister before I came to the island. Because of that, I understood how hard it was for most people to toss an object like a knife or an axe and hit what they were aiming for.

Ian squatted down and looked at the knife, not touching it. I knew he was a huge fan of movies and television and I had a feeling his latest bingeing experiences included at least one crime drama the way he looked but didn't touch.

"It's fancy," Ian said. He pointed out that the handle was some sort of brushed black metal inset with two red stones.

"Those are magic," Dirk said, kneeling down across from Ian.

"I can feel it," Ian agreed.

I couldn't. But then I mostly noticed spells that were being done. I hadn't ever tried to see if I could tell if something was enchanted.

A dragon-fly buzzed around my head. The little blue dragon landed on my arm and sat there, puffing away. The clover scent reached my nose, overpowering the breakfast smells of coffee and eggs.

My arm itched where the creature sat, but I had no idea what it would do if I tried to scratch. None had landed on me before.

"They like you," Gretchen said smiling.

"At least this one," I agreed.

"They rarely settle on a person. The last person, I think, was Darla. Maybe it has something to do with spirit magic?" Gretchen added.

I raised an eyebrow. The dragon-flies had not been pleased to see Darla, or maybe the swarm that had been with her when she'd come into the office had been their way of welcoming her. They hadn't ever swarmed around me, though I knew they'd protected me when the funnel cloud hit.

The door to the B&B opened. My dragon-fly left my arm and flew off to more interesting places. Carl walked into the dining room looking around.

"What have we got?" he asked, squatting down beside Dirk. Carl was a big guy and while Dirk wasn't exactly a small man—in fact, mentally I'd always thought of him and Bill as lumberjacks given their flannel shirts—but he looked like a half-grown teenager next to Carl.

"Stones in the knife are enchanted," Dirk said before Ian could answer.

"It didn't hit me, though," Ian said. "I didn't even have time to think about magic."

"It's the building," Carl said.

Ian nodded. "Normally it doesn't have to protect me, though. I'm usually faster. It was like I was half-asleep, watching her throw it."

I hadn't felt anyone doing a spell. My arms hadn't

tingled until Gretchen had stood up and calmed Ian. I yawned, thinking about it.

My eyelids felt rather heavy and I wished I'd stayed in bed just a little longer. The Eggs Benedict would have still been here.

I started when one of the women seated near the window toppled out of her chair. She got up, her face flaming. The woman with her looked as tired as I felt, only sitting up to look because of the noise.

Dirk yawned and shook his head.

"Spell," Ian whispered.

I hadn't felt it.

Gretchen gulped, looking around at all of us. She didn't seem tired at all. Neither did Carl, but he hadn't been here earlier.

"I bet it was the dragon-fly effect" she muttered. "I tried to just calm Ian, but it looks like everyone got a huge dose of calming. Maybe some tea?"

That made sense. I still wanted to lay my head down and close my eyes. I felt a tingling on my arms, again. But this spell wasn't relaxing. This spell was more of an energetic boost. It was enough to have me sitting upright, in no danger of falling over like the woman by the window.

Ian gave himself a small shake, rather like a dog shaking off a bit of water, and then focused back on the knife. "I can sense Darla, but there's someone else there. Like there's someone possessing her or something," Ian whispered.

He looked up at me. "Holly can you help me?"

"How?" I asked. I was willing to help, but I had no idea how.

"Can you focus on the knife and see if you can see who was with Darla?" Carl asked. "Ian and I can talk you through the relaxation. It's going to require someone with spirit magic and you're the only person on the island that has it. At least that we know of."

"It would take spirit magic to possess Darla, if that's what's going on," Ian said. "I could be wrong. It's possible the dragon-flies are messing with my senses. The knife isn't a person, after all."

"We'll worry about that after Holly checks it out," Carl said.

I laid my hands on my lap and half-closed my eyes. I went through the steps of getting comfortable and focusing. Bernice had taught me many tricks on relaxation. Fortunately, I was awake enough that I wasn't going to fall asleep again. Then I stared at the knife. I made a conscious effort not to change it, but to see it for what it was.

I felt something, but I didn't know what it was. And then I got cold. My body started to shiver hard enough to move the table. The silverware clanked on the plate until someone, probably Gretchen, put a hand out on the plate to stop it.

I focused in on that cold and had a fleeting sense of a woman. I thought I saw Darla but that was all. It was gone.

The air around me warmed. My body no longer felt as if I were in a deep freeze. Whatever I had seen, which was nothing, was gone.

I opened my eyes and shook my head. "I had a sense of Darla and maybe another woman. And then it was gone."

I slumped. I hated that I had failed when knowing what was going on was so important. Of course, I knew I shouldn't be hard on myself for failing the first time I tried to do something. Heaven knew how often Bernice had had to repeat lessons before I got them. This time, though, it wasn't just a lesson. It was something that we needed to know.

"It's okay," Ian said. "I can't read it either and it's in the B&B. Usually I can get something more than I'm getting."

"There's plenty of magic around it," Carl said. "When you were trying to get a read on it, I felt protection magic spiking, blocking other magic. I'm going to take this to the office and I'll work on it with Rose."

He pulled out a pair of gloves and picked up the knife, placing it in an evidence bag, as if we were an ordinary place with ordinary crime.

Ian clapped his hands. "That's all for the show, folks. Get back to your breakfast before it gets cold! We can only keep it at the perfect temperature for so long!"

A few people chuckled. Dirk stood up and walked over to his table. He and Bill finished their coffee and waved at Ian. The B&B would automatically charge them for their food and they'd get a bill at the end of the month. I'm sure there were shop owners who would die for such a convenience at their places of business.

Gretchen watched, sipping her tea. She seemed to be keeping a particular eye on me. For a moment I worried she suspected I knew something, then I realized she was making sure I didn't fall over from having overdone some magic.

I settled in to finish my coffee. I had a stray piece of kiwi in the dish which I chowed down. Doing magic can wipe out your energy and eating anything would help me. It's not like I did spirit magic on a regular basis. Maybe if I did, I'd have been able to figure out what was going on with the knife. I resolved to practice more, though I didn't exactly have a teacher.

"I wouldn't go practicing your spirit magic alone. Especially not under the dragon-fly influence," Gretchen said, appearing to read my mind.

I paused the coffee cup halfway to my mouth, trying to figure out how she knew what I was thinking.

Gretchen smiled. "I'd have worried if you weren't thinking that."

I took a sip. The coffee was still warm, as Ian had promised.

"I know we don't have a spirit magic teacher, but don't go searching for spirits. That can get you into trouble. I'm particularly concerned because there's something strange going on," Gretchen added. "I don't have any spirit magic, but I do know a little about it. Magic in general is so very interesting."

I nodded. She was right. But the idea of practicing now that I'd thought of it, had taken root. It was an idea that wouldn't let go. I knew then that it was going to be a temptation I'd have to fight for the next few weeks, at least.

Chapter Ten

After the excitement of breakfast, I headed to the office. Once at work I forced myself to concentrate on mundane numbers and information. I was distracted so I went over the numbers a second time, making minor corrections. I hoped I wouldn't find more problems later. By the time I set the work aside, it was close enough to lunch that I felt okay about taking a break.

I grabbed a quick bite from the deli in the grocery store. They made nice sandwiches, which went well with a bag of chips. With the sun out, it was quite pleasant outside where a few tables had appeared on the sidewalk. I wasn't the only one enjoying the nice day.

Dragon-flies flitted about, but unlike my cats, none of them tried to poach my sandwich, although one did sniff the chips. I wondered if the little creatures were attracted to salt or if that one was just particularly nosey.

A small group of women sat nearby and gossiped about Darla, though in their tale, Ian had barely survived and she'd grown in her magical power such that she could probably take on Damien. When I glanced over, the discussion stopped abruptly, leaving only the sound of the waves against the shore.

Finishing my lunch, I strolled to the library to talk to Lauren. I knew she took her lunch later. She preferred that, saying it felt to her as if it shortened her late afternoon slump. Besides, plenty of islanders wanted to use the library during their lunch.

I enjoyed the walk, listening to the waves, the sound of which faded into the background just slightly. The women gossiping were still at their table. Perhaps they'd continue to make up stories to scare themselves now that I wasn't there to be shocked by their banter.

The dragon-flies danced around behind me as if I were their personal pied piper. They hadn't done that before and I wondered if it had something to do with me doing more spirit magic.

The library looked like an ordinary two-story office building of brick and wood, although the wood looked fresher and the paint always looked shiny, as if someone had just slapped on a coat and was waiting for it to dry. Another perk of the island. The buildings all looked well-tended and freshly painted. The entry to the library was a large tiled area with a place to hang coats and jackets in the winter. There was even a bench if you came in with snow boots that you wanted to change.

Once through the entry, I stepped onto plush burgundy carpet. Lauren sat encircled by a large rounded desk. Beyond that, shelving ran towards the walls, almost like spokes on a wheel, though the main part of the building wasn't round. To my right was a stairwell to the second floor and tucked in behind was an elevator, which, though small, moved quickly and quietly. The library near my sister's home had a clunky elevator that gasped and whined its way up and down the three-story building so slowly that it seemed like you were always just one breath away from being stuck inside for hours, waiting on rescue.

Lauren wore a deep blue scarf around her neck highlighting the blues in her pink and blue blouse. I had a feeling she had on a blue pencil skirt as well and probably blue heels. I often wished for her fashion sense and the ease with which she put outfits together.

"Holly," Lauren said.

"Hey," I waved a little still walking to the desk. I glanced around at a couple of tables scattered between Lauren's desk and the entry, but no one sat at them. The soft music playing in the background didn't quite cover a few thumps as someone marched around upstairs.

"I had a question about everything that's going on," I said. I pulled up a chair that sat towards the back of the desk, in case someone needed to wait on Lauren to get answers.

"Are you sure you shouldn't be talking to Xavier?" Lauren asked first. "Or Ian. He'd know next, right?"

I smiled a little. "It's more like how could what's going on happen? I mean if the island knows us, how can it not know Darla?"

"It would know her. It might not immediately recognize her if her spirit was changed enough, like maybe she was converted to the light side or something," Lauren half-joked.

"But Ian didn't know she was on the island. He knew there was probably someone, but couldn't get a fix on who it was or why they were here," I said.

Lauren nodded. "I heard. It's strange that he wouldn't know that. He ought to. His powers are clearly delineated in some of the older enclave books. I heard a rumor about her being possessed, but that shouldn't have mattered to the Innkeeper. Ian should have picked up on a new person on the island, even if the island didn't know who it was. From what I gather from the gossip, he didn't know anyone else was on the island at all at first?"

I agreed that was the case.

"I looked into that," Lauren said. "Normally, as the Innkeeper, most of Ian's powers shouldn't be subject to the dragon-fly effect. I mean, some of the little stuff, the things he'd be able to do without his bond, might go awry, but knowing who's on the island is part of his bond to the B&B, or as they said in the old days, 'the inn.'"

"Was there anything to explain why he might not know?" I asked.

"Nothing," Lauren said. "Not even with the dragon-fly effect."

"But?" I pressed.

"How did Darla look?" Lauren asked again.

I frowned not certain where she was going. "Like she always did. Red hair, although she'd had it cut and changed the style. Small. She was angry when I saw her the first time. Probably the second time, too, considering she threw a spelled knife at Ian."

"I heard there were protection spells on it so no one has been able to read it. That takes power. And," Lauren wagged a finger at me, "I heard rumors that Xavier called Far Haven and Alexander Milton owned a spelled knife much like the one on the floor."

"I heard Alexander was a powerful mage," I said. Lauren probably knew that if she'd heard everything else.

"That's common knowledge," Lauren agreed, though she did it gently so I didn't feel foolish for bringing it up, though it was pertinent.

"Could he have been killed for the knife?" I wondered out loud. "And why Darla? She was never that powerful."

"But the hints of possession," Lauren said. "It means it

could be someone else. Someone from the past. When Damien was cut off from the island, the spirits he'd held were all released. It's certainly possible a mage with spirit magic might be trying to harness those spirits, though most would have moved on by now."

"But why would Alexander come here? He didn't have spirit magic, did he? Wouldn't other people go looking for another rogue mage? He was supposed to be watching Damien." I felt frustrated that there were so many pieces but no real answers.

Lauren rested both arms on the desk, hands together, like a particularly good student. She studied her fingers for a bit.

"After Damien, I did some looking into the enclave history. Not just ours, of course. Damien wasn't the first mage to want power and immortality. I mean, Damien wasn't even really a mage, exactly. But just because we have to accept ourselves doesn't mean we always accept others or that we don't have insecurities. There have been other mages that have tried to harness the power of the enclave and failed."

"Even Sharon…" I pointed out.

Lauren nodded. "Even Sharon. And she'd have reason to be upset about Damien not succeeding and being taken off island."

"But she's dead," I said. "Don't spirits, like…learn things?"

Lauren made a face and shrugged. "Don't look at me. I'm just the librarian. You're the one with spirit magic. Given that the spirits helped you with Sharon and Damien, I suspect sometimes they hang around."

"It's not like I sat down and talked to them about what happens in the afterlife," I said, "But yes, spirits were there to help. So at least some stick around, though I couldn't say why or who or how. Given that Damien taught me virtually nothing and now no one with spirit magic is here to help me. I'm not exactly an expert."

I hated the way that last sounded. Almost a whine. But it was frustrating to realize how little I knew. I needed more information.

Lauren nodded. "It's frustrating for about the first year. Then you start learning what questions to ask. It's not like we don't want to teach newbies, no matter how Bernice comes across, it's just that there's so much and it can be difficult to know what people have figured out and what they haven't."

She was right.

"I'm just learning that Ian is the Innkeeper. I feel like everyone knew that but me. And then the stuff about Alexander Milton being so powerful and it's common knowledge..." I trailed off.

"I mean, the Milton thing might be common knowledge, but only to those who pay attention. Even in the outside world, I bet you didn't pay attention to all aspects of the news. The same is true here. I suspect, though, after what happened with Damien, more people are paying attention to what goes on in the enclaves and how to protect themselves. No one wants to think they've done something against their will.," Lauren said.

"But Bernice knew and she was still spelled," I said.

Lauren nodded. "Partly. The U Council thought that Xavier might be able to spell himself and hold Damien off. When he failed, they helped Bernice put spells on so that Damien wouldn't notice. I looked into it and it appears that what failed Xavier is that Damien noticed the spells and could work around them."

"You looked a lot of things up," I said.

Lauren grinned. "I love information. And, to be

honest, the whole magic thing interests me. I want to know everything about it. It's not just finding the information for someone else, I want to know and learn. I'm incredibly jealous that you have spirit magic. Mine is all air and earth with a bit of fire. I don't think I could shift water if my life depended upon it."

"I'm not sure how useful spirit magic is to me, though. Like I said, there's no one to teach me so I don't know how to use it. And now, with the dragon-flies…which reminds me, Gretchen said they seem attracted to people with spirit magic, have you learned anything about that?"

"Oh yeah. I read that some people with particularly strong spirit magic can even speak with them," Lauren said.

"I haven't managed that, but they do seem to want to follow me around now," I said. "And having done a little spirit magic at Carl and Ian's request this morning, they seem even more interested in me."

"Try talking to them and asking them questions," Lauren said. "I hear they'll tell the truth, although it might not be exactly what you're looking for. Like asking if they'll be working on Tuesday and they say yes. They'll be working, but perhaps not at what you thought they'd be doing and that kind of thing."

"Kind of like talking to fairies," I said.

"Maybe not quite." Lauren tapped her fingers and looked to one side. "They won't be mean about it and I always had the sense that fairies were a little mean. The dragon-flies just don't think like we do and can be very literal."

I made a note to start trying to talk to the dragon-flies. Maybe not about anything important at first. Not until I figured out how they responded. Maybe I'd start with questions I already knew the answer to.

Lauren looked up after she finished talking. I turned around. Jack was hurrying into the library, looking to his right and left, as if he was afraid of being seen. When he finally looked straight ahead and spotted me, he nodded. I was clearly the person he was looking for.

"What is it?" I asked when he got there.

"Xavier wants to speak to you about Darla. He sounds serious. Like it's bad," Jack said. He practically bounced from foot to foot.

"Go on and get some lunch," Lauren told Jack. "Holly will head over to the police station."

Jack nodded and then glanced behind him. He scurried away, like he wanted to hide in the stacks. Lauren and I exchanged a look.

Moments later, Xavier marched into the library, his mouth set in a hard line. Bernice followed him, looking as worried as I'd ever seen her.

Chapter Eleven

Xavier marched over to me. His feet hit the plush carpet so hard, I felt the floor move just a tiny bit. I watched and felt myself swallow in anticipation of something bad. My stomach turned in knots.

"Where were you for the last twenty minutes?" Xavier asked.

"I walked over here and talked to Lauren," I said. I tried to remember if anyone had seen me coming this way. I'd chatted with Patti while she made my sandwich. And, of course, the table of women had seen me eating. Too bad I didn't know any of their names.

"Is that true?" Xavier looked at Lauren.

"She's been here at least fifteen minutes," Lauren said. "If she left her office before that, it would take at least five minutes to walk here."

"She left, according to Jack," Xavier said, "Fifteen minutes before that."

"I stopped at the deli and had a sandwich. Patti waited on me," I filled in. "I ate out at one of the tables. A group of women was sitting around talking. I know they saw me."

"I'll ask David," Bernice said quietly. "He often looks out his window and he's just across the street. He'll probably know who the women are, though I bet Florence Ann was part of the group. She usually eats there."

She turned to go, but Xavier shook his head and gave Bernice a warning. "I don't need you doing police work. Not on this. You're too close."

"What exactly is this?" I asked while Bernice glowered at Xavier for his comment.

"Someone saw you chasing Darla down the beach. Darla disappeared, we're not sure where. It happened about twenty minutes ago." Xavier watched for my reaction.

"But I haven't been down at the beach today at all. Not any of the beaches."

"Check her shoes," Lauren said. "You can never quite get the sand off the shoes."

"Magic," Xavier said, not bothering to look.

Bernice snorted. "Look. It's not like her cleaning magic is all that good at the best of times. I expect with the dragon-fly effect, it's worse."

Despite Xavier's skepticism, I took off my shoes. They were sensible enough, rubber-soled things like ballet flats but with support. They wouldn't have been my first choice for either running or walking on the beach, though they wouldn't have made it impossible to do so.

Xavier looked them over and handed them back. "Not proof."

"She wasn't sweaty or breathing hard when she got here," Lauren said quietly. "I am good with details like that."

Xavier looked me up and down. "Then who the hell did Gretchen see?"

I had no idea.

"She said she didn't notice magic," Bernice said. "I went down to the beach, near where she said you were running, but I didn't see anyone. It's like you both disappeared."

"Dragon-flies," Lauren said. "Maybe it hasn't happened yet?"

I hoped she was wrong. I had no desire to go running along the beach after Darla.

"But where would she have gone?" I asked. "Are there caves around there?" I knew the island had plenty of caves but I hadn't heard about an entrance near the office.

"There are caves where the island wants caves," Bernice said. "I didn't notice anything when I was there and I should have. Even with the dragon-fly effect, I should have, if there had been caves for her to enter. We're concerned that she fell into the lake and drowned."

"Who would drive her to do that? In fact," I said, "I was reading last night that someone broke into her hotel room when she was in Tucson. Could someone have been driving her here?"

Xavier raised an eyebrow. "Why?"

"That is the question," I said.

"I'll still need you to come to the station. I have some spells I can do to make sure you're telling the truth about not chasing her. At least not yet," Xavier said.

I waved at Lauren as we left. She looked perplexed. Once out the door, the dragon-flies immediately swarmed around me.

"They like you," Bernice observed.

"Lauren thinks it's because I've just recently tried using my spirit magic," I said.

Bernice gave me a sidelong glance.

"Carl and Ian asked me to try and see if someone was

possessing Darla because of what they sensed on the knife," I said.

Xavier turned and looked at me. "Have you ever astral projected? I hear that takes spirit magic."

I shook my head.

"No one here has any clue how to teach her," Bernice said. "I've considered having her visit Western Jewel. They have several people who teach spirit magic there."

This was the first I'd heard of that. I had no idea where Western Jewel was. I had only the vaguest idea of where any of the enclaves were. Even living on Jewel, I couldn't have pointed to it on a map. Though I knew it was somewhere in Lake Michigan, towards the southern part.

Xavier sighed. "Well let's get you to the station. Bernice and Carl and I can examine you magically to be sure that wasn't you on the beach. Given that Lauren can vouch for you for most of the time frame and chances are someone saw you at the deli, it leads me to believe you, but I need to have this solid. Too much has gone on with Darla and someone who claims to be you."

I realized that Xavier was right. Someone had called Darla and claimed to be me, getting her fired from her job at Hidden Rock. Now, someone who looked like me had chased her along the beach. Whatever was going on, it seemed as if I were in the middle of it and I didn't like it one bit.

Bernice patted me on the arm, a surprisingly kind thing for her to do. I glanced over at her.

"I don't like this," she said keeping her voice low. "This stinks of Damien, but for the life of me I can't figure out how. He's still in Far Haven. And while Alexander Milton might have been the strongest of the mages there, he was far from the only one powerful enough to keep an eye on rogue mages."

I had to agree with her, based on what I knew.

"I hear you," Xavier said. We were nearly to the station and I noticed the white clouds floating in and beginning to cover the blue skies. They didn't seem like rain clouds, but they were making the day seem far less bright.

Bernice said nothing further. She walked faster than either Xavier or me and she led the way, her back as straight as a marine at attention.

I kept up with Xavier just fine, although he didn't talk to me as we finished our walk. It made me vaguely uncomfortable. The dragon-flies flitted around behind me, staying close, but not so close that they were annoying.

I remembered that Xavier had liked Sharon and I'd killed her. Of course, I'd liked Sharon, too, and technically, I had just sent her magic back to her and she hadn't been able to, what Ian called, "catch it."

Xavier held the glass door to the station open for me. It wasn't a large building. The entry had several ugly and uncomfortable looking plastic chairs with metal legs. A few feet away a large brown counter divided the space. Rose moved around behind it, her head bobbling around like it was about to fall off at any moment.

Bernice paused by the low swinging gate that allowed access to the back. Rose moved quickly over there, fumbling with a latch so that Bernice could go through and waited while we all passed through to the back, her head bobbing all the time.

Xavier walked past his desk which sat next to the window on the left. Carl's desk was there too. Another desk sat beyond his, which I knew belonged to another of the police officers, though I didn't know her well. I'd only ever seen her around. I tried to decide if I preferred that it was Xavier and Carl trying to find out if I were lying or if I'd have preferred someone I didn't know at all.

In the main part of the office, away from the windows a large area was filled with tables behind which were file cabinets. Xavier walked through a door beyond the file cabinets. I had visions of a row of cells or an interrogation room that stank of urine and cigarettes.

While we were led into a hallway, the room Xavier led me into didn't smell of anything but faint traces of a floral perfume. Several comfortable looking gray club chairs sat around in a circle, close enough that even Xavier, thin as he was, had to push a couple aside to step between them. He gestured to one that would put my back to the door.

I settled in, only a little worried that I would be too wide to be comfortable. But like everywhere else on the island, the chair accommodated my wide hips and thighs and it was a comfortable seat. Bernice took the chair across from me and Xavier sat beside me.

The two of them held hands over the arms of their chairs. They clearly knew what they were doing.

"Close your eyes," Bernice ordered.

I did so.

"I need you to clear your mind. Pretend like you're going to work some magic with me and just meditate on nothing at all."

I focused on my breath, letting my thoughts go. At one time this would have been more difficult, but I'd become used to clearing my mind in the months I'd lived on Jewel. My body relaxed. I heard the faint sounds of Rose moving around in the front of the office as the floors squeaked. A drawer closed.

Bernice and Xavier were breathing deeply in unison and I could track their breaths. I matched mine to theirs without a second thought. It seemed natural to do so.

My arms tingled when they started working their magic.

The tingling became an itch, which was new. Usually, it just began to hurt. But this itched. I wondered if I were allowed to move but quickly pushed that thought away and tried to concentrate on my breathing and keeping my mind clear.

My head began to feel achy and heavy. It wasn't quite a headache but more like I could be getting a headache. I waited for the pain to increase but it didn't. My head just felt heavy. So heavy, in fact, that I wasn't sure my neck could hold it up.

My chest began to feel tight. The itchiness became a burning that flowed down my arm like a small trail of lava. Outside I heard a sort of animal scream. Just once and it stopped. My eyes popped open.

Bernice was staring at me.

"Well, it was definitely not you out there on the beach," she said.

Xavier opened his eyes. "No. It wasn't. But the dragon-flies were there in your head along with us. And they weren't happy with us checking to make sure you were telling the truth. One tried to attack me. I fought back. I think that was the scream we heard."

I hated that even one of the little dragon-flies might have been harmed because of me. I hated that they might have been harmed anyway.

Bernice leaned forward. "I've never heard of the creatures being hurt before. Or making a sound."

I hoped that the fact that no one had harmed them before meant they couldn't be. I had always thought of dragons as indestructible. I worried about the dragon-flies. I didn't want to go out of the police station and find one dead on the ground.

Xavier and Bernice leaned back. Carl peeked in, his timing impeccable or else he had been roped into the spell in some way. Finding us sitting around, he came in with food and drink for everyone.

I stood up and left the room. No one complained or tried to stop me. Rose watched me leave the building, but said nothing.

Outside, dragon-flies were flying around with a speed that I hadn't noticed before. They almost seemed anxious. I looked around. There, on the ground was a single dragon-fly. I walked towards it, dreading that it might be dead. My heart leapt when I saw it move slightly. I knelt down near it and picked it up.

I had thought the dragon-flies would feel warm but this one felt cool in my hand. It was a blue one. The little creature looked at me and gave a single puff of smoke before laying its head down like it was too weak to hold it up. Another dragon-fly landed on my hand nearby. It held a tiny bit of grass or something and fed it to its weakened friend, completely ignoring me except for my hand which offered them a platform upon which to sit.

The second dragon-fly flew off to join the anxiously dancing group nearby. A red dragon-fly showed up and fed the little blue another tiny bit of vegetation. It was long and thin like grass, though it could have been ripped from part of a leaf.

The blue ate and the red flew off, joining the dancing group. This repeated with different colored dragon-flies landing on my palm to feed the little blue and then dancing away. Slowly the dragon-flies slowed to a more normal flying speed. A couple buzzed around my head, leaving behind the traces of clover scent.

Bernice left the station. A couple of dragon-flies flew around her head, making her stop. One leaned in, almost as if it was smelling her while its wings went a million miles an hour—hummingbirds had nothing on these creatures—

but seeming satisfied, it left. The others went back to their own dance a little out of the way.

"It's letting you hold it?" Bernice asked.

"It was lying on the ground. It seems weak," I said.

The little blue made a liar out of me by standing up and staring at Bernice. It puffed a bit of smoke and even sent out a tiny thread of flame towards her. I felt the heat on my hand, more than I expected from such a tiny flame. My fingers reddened a bit but quickly went back to their usual pale color.

"I've never seen one that even appeared to be hurt," Bernice said. "I wonder why it happened. I saw it around you, like Xavier, but I didn't see it connected in any way. And I didn't get the feeling it was attacking him. It just flew towards him which they tend to do when they're curious."

"I don't either," I said. "I wish I knew what it was doing. Can you tell me?" I asked the dragon-fly.

A chill came over me, rather like the feeling I got if I were talking to a ghost. "I can." I heard the voice around me, as if the very earth were speaking all over.

I looked at Bernice. She didn't look as if she'd heard a thing.

"I got a response," I said. "It said it can tell me."

Bernice almost raised an eyebrow indicating interest. "Then perhaps ask it. Then maybe see if it knows about Darla."

"What were you doing when Xavier saw you via the spell?" I asked. I tried to be as specific as I could, though no doubt I'd forgotten something. I remembered what Lauren said about dragon-flies being very literal.

"I was protecting you," it said.

"What from?" I asked. I hoped that was specific enough. The chill remained and my hand started to feel cold enough that the little dragon didn't seem quite as comfortable, walking up onto the sleeve of my shirt as if the chill of my skin bothered it.

"The invisible one."

"Who is the invisible one?"

"She ran the island," it said.

I started to shiver. I was really cold. When I'd talked to ghosts, I immediately got really cold, but I didn't keep getting colder and colder like I was with the dragon-flies.

"Why did I need to be protected from her?"

"So you are not harmed." The dragon-fly said it as if I were an idiot for not knowing that. Perhaps I was. Or maybe it was my brain getting too cold to think of reasonable questions that could be asked.

"Thank you," I told it. I let it sit on me, but stopped focusing on the dragon-fly, hoping the chill would dissipate. The cold seemed to leave slightly, but by that time I felt chilled through and didn't know if I'd ever get warm again.

"I need to head back to the office," I said. "I'm freezing. Apparently talking to dragon-flies is a lot like talking to ghosts in that it's cold."

"What did it say?" Bernice asked. She started walking at her usual pace.

I kept my arm up, which was a bit awkward but I didn't want the blue to get hurt if I moved and it slid off my hand.

"That it was protecting me from the invisible one who used to run the island," I said.

Bernice said nothing for a moment. "Did it give a name?"

I shook my head. Of course, Bernice was ahead of me so she didn't see it. I saw the pause and the turn, waiting for a response.

"No." I said.

"There was one person here who ran the island long ago, who used a spell that turned them invisible. It took years to undo it. Although from the books I've read they rather liked the ability to spy. They were known as the unseen mayor. I suppose it might be referring to that person. Or maybe a ghost, like Sharon," Bernice said. "What with Darla and all, I'm inclined to think of the latter."

I had to agree with Bernice. Sharon was the first person who had come to mind for me, too. I mean, she wasn't invisible but she was dead and possibly a ghost. Add that to the possibility of Darla being possessed and me being a target, and Sharon seemed like a good fit .

Bernice sighed. "I'll make some calls and see if there's someone with spirit magic who is available to come to the island. We definitely need an expert, and while you have power, you haven't been trained. That can be a dangerous thing, especially if you're the target of a spirit with malevolent intent."

Only Bernice could say that with a straight face. I'd have laughed if my stomach hadn't sunk down to my toes. I looked at my tiny protector and hoped that they would be enough.

Chapter Twelve

By the time I got to the accounting office, my little dragon-fly friend had flitted off to join the others. While the tiny creatures flew around me, they stayed mostly behind me so as not to trouble my walk. They also stayed further away than typical, probably because I was cold enough to have emitted as much chill as a block of ice.

Despite Bernice's quick pace and the bright sunshine, I was still shivering when I got inside. I had no idea how I'd get any work done. Jack poked his head timidly out of his door. I smelled tuna salad, which he'd probably gotten at the deli for lunch. My sandwich had been better.

"You're okay?" Jack asked.

"Just cold. I talked to one of the dragon-flies and I got really chilled." I looked longingly at the fireplace. It was gas so I didn't have to bring in wood to light the fire, but it still took a bit to warm up. My office was normally at a temperature that was comfortable for me.

As I watched, the fireplace came on, as if nudged by my thoughts, or perhaps I was cooling the room down so much that its thermostat kicked it on. I didn't hesitate to stand in front of it, rubbing my arms, trying to get circulation going. I realized I still had goosebumps, too.

My teeth didn't quite chatter, but it had been a near thing walking behind Bernice.

"Did you always get that cold talking to ghosts?" Jack asked.

"I don't think so. With the dragon-flies, I kept getting colder. The ghosts were cold, but it was like you just got cold next to them, like walking into a freezer. I kept getting colder with every question I asked of the dragon-flies."

Jack nodded, thoughtfully. "Interesting. I don't understand much about spirit magic. Just enough to be thankful I don't have it. It seems like it's too much. I'd want to know too many things and the temptation to ask for information I don't need to have, to pry, you know, would be too much."

He looked down at his shoes as if he'd said too much. I had to admit, as much as I hated what was going on with Darla, the fact that Jack seemed to be coming out of his shell was a plus.

"I don't know how to use my magic, so it hasn't really been a temptation. And the one time I did use it, the spirits came to me. I guess things like that just didn't occur to me. I suppose if someone were teaching me, it might be more tempting to ask about stuff that maybe I shouldn't know…" I let that trail off thinking. I had no real desire to know what the dead knew.

I suppose it might be nice to communicate with the people I loved who had passed. I could tell my grandmother that I loved her and maybe ask her for some family history, but it wasn't like I wanted to know secrets about people here or anything.

I shivered again, stepping a little closer to the fire, which was warmer than I thought it should be now that it was going. The island had probably done that. I was surprised it hadn't just warmed up the room. Of course, Jack was in the room, too, and the island wouldn't want to make him too warm.

"If I go in my office, do you think the island will heat my office more so that I can warm up, but you won't be too hot?" I asked Jack.

Jack looked around, almost surprised that I'd asked him a question, though why he would be I didn't know. We talked about bookkeeping and accounting all the time.

"I think so, yeah," he finally said.

I stepped away from the fire and headed to my office. I hated to leave it. I loved the feel of it on my back. Almost as soon as I stepped away, the fire went out. I hurried to my office, walking almost as fast as Bernice. It was warmer in there and heat came down through the upper vent over my desk. I almost sighed.

Oddly, Jack followed me into my office, which meant the heat from the vent wasn't quite as warm.

"Are you sure you'll be okay?" he asked. "Xavier looked really upset. I guess someone saw you chasing Darla?"

"It wasn't me. Xavier and Bernice did a spell to check that," I said.

"That's good," Jack said. "I told them you couldn't do that, but no one listens to me." He gave a sort of huff and left the room. It hadn't quite sounded self-pityingly, just an honest assessment of how people treated him. I knew I had and I wished I'd done better. Jack was clearly more perceptive than I gave him credit for.

Next time I talked to Ian, I'd ask him if he knew how perceptive Jack was. Ian seemed to know everything, and those things he didn't know, he appreciated hearing about.

I should have asked Lauren for a book on the various

island powers that might help me understand things like the title "Innkeeper." If every enclave had an Innkeeper, then no doubt it was mentioned in a book somewhere. In fact, such a topic probably had its own book. I decided to look online to see if I could learn anything.

Maybe there was a magical way to let witches find certain websites that ordinaries weren't supposed to get access to. I mean, they had put up a job posting that only potential witches would see. There had to be sites that didn't seem to exist to anyone but those with power.

Settling in to do some searching, I pushed the guilt that I wasn't actually working to the back of my mind, telling myself I'd get to it once I'd warmed up again and my hands weren't a wee bit shaky.

Chapter Thirteen

I shouldn't have been surprised to actually find information. It took a little doing. I had to add "enclave" and then a colon to all of my searches about mages, but once that was done, I brought up plenty of information. By the time I was finished, I was warm and didn't feel too much guilt about not working on the things on my desk.

I had some forms to mail out for some of the businesses and a few items to update in the computer. It would take me maybe an hour, less if I hurried and didn't run into trouble. I started working on those things while I tried to digest what I'd learned.

Ian's powers would continue to grow as time went on. The bond between him and the B&B was more symbiotic than anything. He would age more slowly. While I'd always thought he looked young, he'd be looking like he was in his twenties or thirties for quite some time. It made sense. He'd been on the island for a good decade and he barely looked thirty. He'd laughed it off, saying he'd always looked young.

I wondered how much he knew about what was happening. The longer he stayed as the Innkeeper and the older he got, the less human he'd become. An Innkeeper's death was different from a normal death. His body would deteriorate and his spirit would become part of the B&B. It said nothing about whether or not Ian had a choice in the matter. I vaguely remembered the ghosts on the island telling Sharon something about her spirit remaining on the island had she died there naturally. Given what I knew about ghost stories, which was far too much considering the situations I found myself in, having been killed, however accidentally, it seemed even more likely that she was still here.

There were other special powers. The mayor had a special attunement to the island. There was actually a ceremony to create that bond. While the mayor would have greater powers to enforce the laws of the enclave, they weren't permanent powers and would be rescinded when a new ceremony took place, installing a new mayor.

As acting mayor, Bernice would have gone through a shorter ceremony which gave her some of the mayoral powers, but not all. When we had the next official election, I suspected Bernice would win. It wasn't like anyone else had said they were interested. After what had happened with Sharon and Damien, no one seemed interested in running the island.

Another special power was given to the person who took on the job of teaching new mages. Like being the Innkeeper, those powers grew. They weren't nearly as impressive in terms of the ability to use the magic of the enclave, but it did let them know when there was a new mage in the enclave, or even if a potential mage was nearby.

Apparently, older teachers sometimes went out and recruited those who were coming into their powers. This wasn't unlike the way I'd been recruited. However, teachers just recruited anyone, whether the enclave had a need of their talents or not. I had a hard time seeing Bernice doing this sort of work, though she had been Jewel's teacher for a nearly a decade when I arrived.

Then there were people like me, who could see spirits and, on rare occasions, speak to them. This wasn't considered a blessing. Rather, this power was labeled as dangerous. Side effects, which was how they were labeled—and that would have given me a chuckle if they weren't talking about me—included being easily possessed, a greater propensity towards dementia, seizures, and spending years in a catatonic state.

None of these sounded very encouraging which is what had made me switch to doing my regular work. I hoped the mundane aspects of my job would ward off seizures and catatonic states and perhaps bore any spirit wishing to possess me. The detail work would keep my brain active, which is said to assist in avoiding dementia, too.

The sunlight was turning pink and the lake had long golden shadows upon the water when I heard Jack moving around to go home. I'd played hooky in the afternoon, mentally, at least. I needed to stay at the office and finish my work. Fortunately, there wasn't much more to do.

A few emails had come in which I answered as the front door closed. The office got quiet. While the heater still blew heat, hissing a bit as it did so, and the refrigerator in the little kitchen dropped some ice from the ice maker, the building felt empty, except for me.

Then suddenly it didn't feel empty at all.

A sound came from the front room. A squeak of the wood floor as if someone had walked into the reception area. I heard something that sounded like someone mumbling, though I knew no one should be out there. The front door makes a distinctive sound. No one was quiet enough to come in without me knowing.

My phone sat on the corner of the desk on my charger. I picked it up, but hesitated to call the police. I didn't want to look foolish because I didn't recognize ordinary evening sounds in my office. I'd spent plenty of late nights there, though, doing taxes. I was often alone. The building didn't make the noises I was hearing.

Still, there was that part of me that didn't want to be the girl who cried wolf thinking someone had snuck in. Besides, even if someone were there, they clearly weren't doing anything.

I pocketed the phone and stood up as quietly as I could. Perhaps because I was thinking about quiet, the building accommodated me. The chair didn't make even the tiniest of squeaks when I stood up. The floor boards didn't creak, though there was an area near the door to my office that sometimes made a sound if you stepped wrong.

Pausing there, I drew in a breath and prepared myself. I readied a protection spell in case someone wanted to hurt me. My hands began to sweat and my stomach churned, tying itself in knots. My heart beat too quickly.

I slipped through the door and turned to face the reception area in one movement only to find Darla standing in the middle of the main room.

She looked as if she were waiting for me, her eyes sharp. She looked worried even as she threw up her hands.

I had my protection spell up before she'd even finished what she was doing.

A deluge of water spewed towards me. It would have knocked me flat, or worse, if I hadn't had the protection up. Some spells allowed water to be animated by the will of the user. If Darla had done one of those, she could force the water to crawl down my throat and hold it there until I drowned in the doorway of my office.

Tears streamed down her face and she crumpled.

"She made me do it," she whispered.

I frowned.

"Who?" I asked.

Darla's eyes hardened again and this time air hit my protection spell. Once, a second spell, particularly a spell in an element I'm not good with, would have torn my shield apart.

Now, though, I'd been well-trained in protection spells. After what had happened to me with Damien and Sharon, I'd wanted to learn them and Bernice had more than accommodated my request. Perhaps she'd had an inkling that I'd need that sort of training more than most people on the island. Or maybe it was just her way of thanking me for helping her rid the island of Damien.

This time Darla bent over, hugging her middle. She stood up again and screamed. More tears fell. Her hands came up around her head.

My head began to pound.

Dragon-flies appeared. The door hadn't opened. The windows were closed. Yet, somehow, I was suddenly surrounded by dragon-flies of all colors. The pounding in my head got worse, first thumps from the left side and then the right. I felt as if someone had put a heavy helmet on my skull and long spikes were being driven into my brain. Not satisfied with that pain, they continued to pound on the spiked helmet attempting to drive those spikes in deeper and deeper. The image was so strong, I worried the pain would kill me.

My hands came up around my ears and I closed my eyes.

I had an image of a field of clover. A particularly large

dragon, not a dragon-fly, lay in the field. It looked at me with enormous orange eyes. It gave a single puff of smoke.

The pounding in my head disappeared as if it had never been.

My hands dropped. I stood straighter.

My eyes opened.

Darla was gone.

Chapter Fourteen

I felt shaky after that.

The dragon-flies were still in the office flitting about, but they weren't all gathered around me like doctors examining a patient. Now they seemed to be exploring. At first, I thought they were looking for Darla, but the way they flitted about, they reminded me more of a curious cat. They appeared to have to sniff everything, occasionally letting out a puff of smoke.

One blew out a thread of fire at the fireplace and seemed perplexed that nothing happened. I wondered how much they understood about the way people lived.

My stomach stopped churning in fear, though my heart still beat too fast. At least it wasn't beating so hard. I was still shaky, but knew I just needed food. While I had hoped to finish more work, it was after hours. I could go to Derry's without feeling too guilty. As Scarlett O'Hara said, tomorrow was another day.

I grabbed my things and left the office, waiting at the door until the dragon-flies—or at least as many as I was aware of—

had flown out. It took longer than I'd have liked. When I finally closed the door and locked it, I figured that since they'd managed to pop into the office to help when everything was closed up, any left behind would be able to get out.

My knees shook as I walked over to Derry's. The dragon-flies continued to follow me like a flock of sheep behind a shepherd. In fact, there were shepherds who would love to keep a flock in such order. The low buzz of their wings mingled with the lap of waves and the usual smell of the lake. The scent of clover that followed the creatures mingled with the lake smell to create an aroma that reminded me of going out to play before the dew had quite dissipated from the lawn. Thinking back, it might have been because our yard had always had as much clover as grass. My father had not been very particular about how his yard looked. He just wanted a green space for his girls to play.

The door to Derry's always looked too narrow to me. When I'd first seen it, I wasn't completely sure even an average-sized person would have fit through, much less a large woman like myself. The little entry area wasn't much wider but all I needed to do was set foot on the first step and I'd be transported up to the restaurant.

Except this time nothing happened. The wood remained beneath my foot. I remained in the little entry area.

I frowned. I stepped back into the entry, feeling a bit claustrophobic. The door had the only window. The walls themselves were painted brick.

The stairs looked as they always did, a flight of wooden steps going up to a second floor. They were narrow and steep. I knew that if I climbed them I wouldn't end up at the restaurant. That took magic.

I put my hand on the bannister and placed my foot on the step. Nothing.

I stepped up with the other foot. Still nothing.

I climbed to the second step. I thought I heard something upstairs but I wasn't transported to the restaurant.

I climbed back down. I left the building. The dragon-flies were hovering around outside.

"Do you know why the magic isn't working?" I asked them. I didn't exactly expect an answer. It was more a rhetorical question. I noticed Tania and Brenden walking down the street. They lived in my complex.

A chill slammed into my body.

"We don't want you to leave us!" The voice came from everywhere and nowhere. Given how I suddenly felt as if I'd jumped into Lake Michigan in January, it had to have been the dragon-flies.

"I'm not leaving you. I'm just getting food." I said.

They swarmed and swirled, but then backed off a bit. I went back into Derry's. This time when I stepped onto the stairs, I was transported up to the restaurant.

Tonight, it wore its Italian bistro theme with white table cloths and dark wood. Wine bottles sat in the center of the table and the napkins were red and white checked. The floor was dark tile. Mindy, the waitress, waved at me from where she was picking up drinks at the bar.

An older man nodded at me and led me to a table near the back. While the chairs mostly had arms, this one didn't. Like always, the seat was wide enough for my hips and accommodated me comfortably.

I settled in to look at the menu which was in a dark cloth folder with sheets of weathered looking paper. The items were written in italics and grapevines decorated the edges. Naturally, Italian dishes were featured, though other options appeared below as I considered what I might want to eat.

Garlic infused the air and in a few minutes Mindy came by with a basket of garlic bread and some water.

"Everything okay?" she asked.

"Fine," I said. She normally didn't ask how I was so I added, "Why?"

Mindy sighed and looked around. "Ten minutes ago we were the steak house and then it just changed around people to the Italian bistro. That was so weird. Probably the dragon-fly effect, but it's thrown a number of people."

"I couldn't get up the stairs a few minutes ago," I said. "Maybe that was why."

"Shouldn't have been, but then if it was the dragon-fly effect, it might have. Do you need some time?" Mindy was pretty no-nonsense. She was one of the few people Sharon hadn't seemed to have liked. It had put me off her at first, but given that Sharon had tried to kill me, that judgement didn't exactly hold the weight it once had.

I glanced at the menu. Chicken Marsala jumped out at me and I asked for that with a side of noodles and browned butter and the Caesar salad. My stomach growled in approval.

"Been using magic then," Mindy said, a bit of approval in her voice.

"I have." I leaned forward on the table, letting my elbows rest. I knew some of the people in the restaurant by name. A few I recognized by their faces, but there were others I didn't recognize at all. I was used to that. Sort of. I mean, I was used to not knowing everyone, but it surprised me that there were still people on the island I didn't at least recognize in passing. Jewel wasn't that big, so far as I knew.

I wolfed down my food as if I were starving, but it helped my shakiness and I felt more myself. As I was finishing, Lauren came in, by herself. She nodded at me and came over to my table, seating herself without asking.

"What's up?" I asked. I mean, we were friends, but not close friends.

"Darla came to the library this afternoon, just as I was getting ready to close. She threw spells at me. Fortunately, elements are not allowed in the library as any of them could harm the books, so nothing was damaged. Then she just disappeared," Lauren said. "I left a bit late because I wanted to check to be sure everything was okay and she wasn't hiding."

"Darla was at my office just after closing, too," I said. "I think Jack left at five and I worked for another few minutes and then I just knew someone was in the office."

"That's the time she was at the library," Lauren frowned. "One of our Darla's definitely wasn't Darla, then."

"Even if it wasn't the exact time, she couldn't have gotten from one place to the other that quickly."

"It's possible to teleport, but really, you need anchors to allow you to do it without expending all your magic. Damien probably had enough to do it, but that's about it." Lauren stopped right there, cocking her head as if in thought.

"What?" I asked. I had finished my dinner. If Lauren was staying I could go for dessert. I used to worry about what people thought of the fat woman with dessert, but I'd gotten more comfortable here. Besides, I'd done magic. I hadn't really gained weight since coming to Jewel Island what with all the walking and the magic.

"Alexander Milton would have had enough magic to do it," Lauren said slowly. "He was that powerful. But it would have left him weaker. Could he have teleported to the ferry, expecting to recuperate here after giving someone information?"

"Isn't that what phones are for?" I asked. We did have good phone service. And considering that the enclaves all had high end electronic stuff—contrary to popular fiction, magic and electronics were perfectly fine together—as well as spells, if someone was worried about another person listening in, there were plenty of countermeasures. In fact, I'd bet that the enclaves had more security than most governments.

Lauren frowned. "Maybe he wanted to be here for some reason? Or perhaps to stop someone else?"

I raised an eyebrow. Mindy came over and asked Lauren what she was having. Lauren took a quick peek at the menu and ordered. She also had a glass of red wine with her dinner.

Mindy took my order for dessert. While I love their tiramisu, I opted for the chocolate lava cake. I wanted something richer and heavier.

"I'll make sure it's a good one for you," Mindy said, taking Lauren's menu and leaving the table.

"Magic?" Lauren asked.

"Darla threw magic at me, so I used protection spells. I had to hold them for a fair amount of time. Weirdly, she seemed conflicted about it. Like she was crying one second and angry and throwing a spell the next."

Lauren's eyebrows drew together.

"She didn't seem quite so conflicted with me. She tried a few spells, but nothing happened… and then she was just gone."

"Did you get a headache from seeing her?" I asked. "I did. Like the worst. The dragon-flies were there and it's like they made it go away."

Lauren stared at me for a moment. "Describe the headache."

The seriousness with which she took my complaint made me go into detail about what I'd felt. I told her as much as I could remember, though, fortunately, the actual pain was already fuzzy around the edges.

"It could have been someone trying to possess you. The fact that the dragon-flies stepped in makes me think that whoever it was wasn't successful. The fact that Darla clearly had a headache, too, lends itself to the belief that she's been possessed. The question, of course, is when that happened and by whom."

Mindy brought Lauren's wine. Lauren picked up the glass, swirled it a bit, watching the colors. She sniffed it and then took a quick sip. Mindy had long since left. Probably, like the rest of the food on the island, the wine would taste exactly how Lauren expected it to and Mindy didn't have to worry about an unhappy customer.

"Maybe when someone went looking for her before she came back to the island," I said.

"That would rule out Sharon. If it were Sharon, the possession would've had to happen on the island," Lauren said.

"I assume to possess someone you'd have to be dead, is that right? I mean, Carl asked if I could astral project which I haven't ever tried. That means I can leave my body, right? Could I take over another body?"

Lauren cocked her head. "I've not thought about it. In theory, I suppose. I'll have to look it up. Possession and astral projection aren't things I've learned much about. While Damien claimed to have spirit magic, and probably did considering he was tapping the island directly, he never used powers like that, not while he was here."

"He couldn't do it from Far Haven, could he?" I realized as I asked, the question was probably foolish. After all, his power had been depleted and not having his own magic meant he couldn't accrue more.

"Damien didn't have his own magic. I think that Alexander and a few others bled the magic Damien had leached from all of us and the island from him before jailing him. He's got small amounts that he can utilize, but not like we do. Accepting our shameful parts increases our abilities to do magic."

"I figured," I said. "Someone killed Alexander, though. Darla wasn't powerful enough to have done it, nor was she big enough to toss his body over the side of the ferry."

"Magic can raise a body and carry it," Lauren said. "That's easy magic. Darla didn't have much other than her spirit magic, but she could probably do that. The thing is, I can't imagine she'd have been able to kill Alexander Milton."

His body was the other piece of the puzzle. Mindy brought out Lauren's order and she dug into her food.

"I'll go back to the library and see what I can find out about Darla being two places at once," Lauren said as she took a bite of the largest chef salad I had ever seen.

"Do you think that's safe? She's already come in there when you were alone." I hated that she might be alone.

"I'd be alone at home, too," Lauren pointed out. "So will you, although you do have the cats. Even so, the island knows us. It wants to protect us. That's always been enough."

"Maybe I ought to come with you? I could call Carl or someone to take me home after," I suggested.

Lauren brushed that off. "I work better alone. I'll be fine."

I hoped she was right.

Chapter Fifteen

No dragon-flies followed me home, but then again, neither did Darla. Sandra, my next-door neighbor was out on her front porch sitting in her white rocking chair. She waved when I got close. I waved back.

A photographer, Sandra did a lot of portraits, which she said was her bread and butter. She also traveled off-island for her work. In fact, I had thought she'd be gone for another day.

"You're home early," I said.

Sandra sighed. She shook her head a little so that her straight black, shoulder length hair moved like a small wave around her head. "I heard there were rumblings on the island and figured it best to get back. I had rented a car, so it wasn't hard to pack it in and come home."

I wasn't sure why she'd need to be here, and that must have shown on my face.

"They've been talking about suspending the ferry service to the island for a few days until this gets figured out. Alexander's death concerns everyone. The U council is planning to visit and once they're here, their word is law. I didn't want to get stuck outside."

"When are they due? I thought Bernice was going to ask someone who does spirit magic to come and help us."

"I'm sure someone on the council has spirit magic. I'm not sure they'll be a personable teacher, but then again, neither was Bernice. Despite that, she got the job done and did it well. I'd say probably better than Gretchen will, for all that Gretchen is nice," Sandra said.

Her voice had a scratchy sound rather like she'd spent a good part of her life smoking.

"I hope they can at least teach me something." I paused and then blurted out, "Darla came to my office at about the same time Lauren saw her in the library."

Sandra made a humph sound and the rocking paused. "I've never heard of someone being able to do that. I have heard that some mages can make it appear someone else is in two places at once, but not themselves. Usually, they make a sort of look-alike of another person and send it off while the actual person goes and does what they want. I guess it's too hard to get your own details correct, so it requires the abilities of another mage. I've studied it a little because it's kind of like a magical walking, talking video or something. Which means, Darla's got to be working with another mage. I heard, though, that Ian didn't sense anyone and only barely got a hint of Darla."

I nodded.

"That's odd," Sandra said. "He knows whenever someone comes on the island. He had a care package from the B&B for me when I got here today. I passed him walking back up the road when I was coming in."

"Whoever it is has to have powerful magic, then."

"Or they're another Innkeeper," Sandra said, nodding. "That would be horrible if one of them went bad."

"How?" I asked. "Isn't their power tied to the inn at their enclave?"

"Of course. But they could take bits of the inns with them, like stationary or a pen or something with the logo. That would have some of the inn's magic. It wouldn't be like being on their home turf, but it helps some of them travel. They don't feel so weak when they leave, which I guess is a huge issue," Sandra said.

"I had no idea," I said.

"You're new. Plus, I travel a lot. More even than Bernice, but she gets information from folks. She talks to them. I just sit around listening. It means I pick up different stuff," Sandra said. "That's good and bad. I mean, no one knows I'm listening, so that's good. But bad because I could have had a protection spell like Bernice's against Damien's magic, but didn't."

Interesting information. Slightly different from what I'd read officially. Of course, did anyone really want super powerful mages running around with small items from their home so they could be powerful anywhere? I mean, it was like a vampire carting around earth from its homeland, which creeped me out. I read and watch far too much horror to be comfortable with the idea. Particularly since I liked Ian.

"Hopefully, Xavier will get this figured out," I said, waving.

Sandra went back to rocking, while I opened my door. It was only then that I realized no dragon-flies were around. Before I'd reached my home, they'd been romping around behind me. Of course, it was nearly dark, so perhaps they had to rest. Maybe they thought Sandra was enough protection. It wasn't as if I was an expert on the behavior of the little things.

Peony and Tulip waited inside for me, both sat facing

the door in the front room like they were there to interro-
gate me about where I'd been.

"What's up?" I asked.

Peony gave a loud meow and ran to me, head-butting
my leg as if I'd been gone for ages. I reached down and
petted her.

Tulip remained in place and yowled at me with the
loud vocalization that only a Siamese cat can make.

I squatted and gestured to her to come over. She came,
slowly, and sniffed at my hand like she wasn't sure I was
me. I hoped I was me. Lauren had recognized me. So had
Sandra, at least as far as I knew.

A chill went down my back. What if the person
chasing Darla had been in here and the cats thought it
was me.

"Was I here earlier?" I asked.

Peony paused in her snuggling to give me a look that
suggested I had asked a stupid question. Maybe I had. The
cats were magic. They'd have known if the person in the
house wasn't actually me.

Too bad I couldn't talk to them. I had once talked to
Ian's cat, Socrates. He'd become a large shadow and had
been able to communicate with us. Peony had never done
that. I wasn't even certain she could. I didn't really understand her powers. Only that she'd appeared in the hospital
on my bed when I'd been healing and had stayed with me
at the B&B while I looked for a home. Once I started
moving in, she'd just appeared in my front room and
settled on the sofa.

A couple of days later, Tulip had joined her and
neither had left since. I fed them regularly. Everyone said
they needed to eat. And eat they did. I also changed litterboxes so while they might be magic, their physical natures
definitely worked like an ordinary cat.

I rubbed both their ears and then stood up. I went to get them their food, hoping that would calm them down.

"What happened, girls?" I asked, moving into my little u-shaped kitchen to get cat food. I opened a new can and spooned it out in their dishes. They still had some of the dry food I left out. Their water fountain had been refreshed that morning.

Neither cat bothered to answer, digging into the food with gusto. Any fears they may have had appeared to be gone now that there was food in their dish. Maybe they were worried that I would get possessed and be unable to come home to feed them. Not that that would be a huge problem. They'd probably just make food appear in their bowls.

Thinking about it, it was too bad they didn't just do magic to clean their own litterboxes. That would be handy. Cats, of course, probably loved seeing their humans on their hands and knees scooping up their leavings.

I stood up and wandered out to my living room. Everything looked normal, but now that the cats weren't distracting me, something felt off. I sniffed the air. It didn't quite smell right. There'd been a scent of clover hanging around the house the last few days. Now it smelled more like cat litter and old cat food, though I'd taken the garbage out that morning and Peony and Tulip rarely left anything out to be eaten.

Frowning, I walked around the place. I sniffed in the first bedroom which I used as my office at home. It had a daybed in there in addition to my desk. The smell was there, but no stronger than in the living room.

I went into my bedroom, dreading what might be there, but nothing. Just the same faint scent. The bathrooms didn't offer up any information. Back in the great room, I wandered over to the kitchen and sniffed around there, but like all smells that you're trying to trace, the fact that I was looking made it harder to detect.

Peony watched from where she was gobbling her food, interested in the fact that I was walking around sniffing at things.

"Was it the smell that bothered you guys?" I asked quietly.

Peony gave a soft mew before turning back to eating. I had no idea if that was an agreement or just a spontaneous display of solidarity.

I went back through my house trying to determine if anything was out of place. I didn't notice anything. If something had been taken, the person knew what to look for. However, the fact that the clover scent was gone seemed more like the dragon-flies might be gone. That bothered me almost as much as the thought of someone in my house. I considered calling Xavier, but I had so little to go on that I doubted there was anything he could do.

I settled in to do some magic to make sure my space was mine. It took just a few minutes and it was a light enough spell that I wasn't immediately famished. The house felt better. The trace scent of clover returned.

I had no idea what had gone on while I was away. The idea that someone had come inside bothered me. The houses were magically protected, though I was still in the habit of locking my doors. Someone who wished me harm shouldn't have been able to come in even if I'd left the door wide open.

Besides that, the cats could protect themselves and would protect me against harm, although the latter was if it suited them. So far, it had suited Peony.

If someone had come in, they couldn't have meant me harm. Or maybe they weren't sure if they meant harm? The ideas swarming through my mind made my head spin.

I settled in on the sofa and pulled up the laptop to start searching out more information on magic. I didn't know enough and now that I knew I could do certain searches to learn things, I wanted to know everything.

Peony settled down next to me and purred. Tulip disappeared into the bedroom.

A few moments later, when I was in the middle of a search about Innkeepers going rogue, a shadow appeared on the wall.

"It wasn't a person who came in," a voice said.

"Socrates?" I asked. Ian's black cat, whom he had named Socrates, had spoken to me in that form once.

"You call me Tulip for some odd human reason," the shadow said.

"What did come in?" I asked.

"It was a spirit, but also had elements of the living. We believe that a spirit of one who has died here has taken on aspects of the spirits of the living," Tulip said. "It is possible our magic has misinformed us, as this spirit seems particularly elusive, as if someone or something else has placed magic on it. The Innkeeper isn't powerful enough to detect the others who are here, but there are three living beings that do not belong here. He will be told of his failure soon enough and be judged for it."

That sounded ominous.

"What do you mean judged for it?"

But the shadow had shrunk to almost nothing and no voice answered my question. But there were three people who didn't belong. I had to guess that Darla was one of them considering she was there and not there. So two others.

One could have made themselves look like me. There weren't spells like in Harry Potter that allowed one to completely look like another person, but between spells to change hair color and the proper clothing, which could easily be spelled, it wouldn't be hard to fool someone from a distance.

Close up was another matter, but if there were spirits involved, then perhaps one had taken Darla's body and another her spirit and made it look like it was real. I'd need to research if such a thing was even possible. Along with finding out what sort of judgements Innkeepers could face.

Chapter Sixteen

I walked to work the next day followed by a battalion of dragon-flies all in formation. When Dirk and Bill had walked out of the B&B after breakfast that morning, they'd laughed to see me.

That was when I'd turned to see the creatures all flying behind me like little soldiers. I'd laughed too. It had felt good. It hadn't been long since we'd found the body on the island and the days had been stressful. Being wrapped up in the intrigue had stolen some of the joy I'd felt since coming to the island and embraced being a mage.

Jack was in the office when I arrived. He looked up and waved, but nothing more. I debated sharing my dragon-fly story, but didn't quite feel comfortable. While I'd learned that he was more perceptive than I had expected, I still wasn't ready to share personal stuff. And for some reason the dragon-flies following me felt personal.

Instead, I headed to my office, just beyond his, and tried to settled into work. When that proved difficult, I texted Ian about lunch. Maybe talking to him would help me work some of this out. Besides, I figured I'd owed it to him to warn him about the judgment that could be coming.

That done, I forced myself to concentrate, though I have to admit to spending more time than I should have staring out the window at the lake. I was thankful that this hadn't happened during tax time or I'd have been in really big trouble.

As I thought about that, a single red dragon-fly flew in front of the window doing a little loop-de-loop and then hovering there looking in for a minute. I smiled. Then it sailed off to wherever they had all gone.

I shook my head, still smiling and got back to work. Finally able to concentrate, the morning passed quickly and before I knew it, Ian was standing in my office waiting.

Today he was dressed in his usual black jeans, white shirt and plaid vest. This was one of his wilder plaids in gold, cream, and black. He'd once told me he only wore it when he was feeling a little down because the bright colors cheered him up. I wasn't sure the vest was exactly bright, but it was definitely cheery and rather more daring than many of his vests.

"What's up?" he asked, as we left the office. Jack was down in the kitchen fixing his lunch so I just yelled out that I was leaving.

"Darla, the dragon-flies, and some stuff I learned from Tulip," I said smiling. I opened the door and was preparing to go through.

Ian paused and looked behind him and then pushed me out. He took my arm and started to pull me up the street. No more easy sashay as if he had all the time in the world.

"What?" I asked, looking back down at Derry's.

"Not here," Ian hissed. He hurried me along.

Once we got to the B&B, the door opened without

anyone having to pull on the latch. Ian hurried me towards the back, where my room had been when I'd stayed there, except now instead of a guest room there was a large space with two sofas. Once we'd entered, a door I hadn't noticed —may not even have existed as we walked in—closed behind us.

Ian closed his eyes. My arms tingled.

"Okay, we're sealed in the B&B," he said. "No one is going to listen in. What do you mean?"

"Why so secretive?" I asked.

"The cats don't just talk randomly. They talk when it's important. And it's typically just information for you, or for you to deliver. I hope you didn't go talking to Jack about it?" Ian said.

"No. But Jack wouldn't…"

Ian shook his head. "That's not the point. The point is, the magic chose to tell you something based on what you know. Are you sure you can even tell me?"

He was sort of scaring me.

"It involved you," I said.

Ian's eye narrowed. "What?"

"Tulip told me there are three people, which, I *think*, includes Darla, on the island, and that the Innkeeper will be judged for not knowing that." It wasn't exactly how she'd phrased it, but it was as close as I could come from memory.

"Three?" Ian gasped. He flopped down on one of the loveseats. Fortunately, it was a plush and overdone thing that caught his weight easily. While the sofas might have been a bland brown, they did look comfortable and I settled on the other one.

"Three," I repeated.

Ian closed his eyes. Magic tingled along my arms. It got stronger and became an itch. I didn't feel any magic coming at me or involving me, so it stayed just an itch which I tried scratching but couldn't quite reach. The sensation felt like ants running up and down my bones deep under my skin. I wanted to shake off the creatures, but shaking out my arms would probably distract Ian from what he was doing.

Finally, the tingling eased. Ian opened his eyes.

"I still can't latch on to the three. I feel Darla. And when I feel her, I recognize her now. There's another person I don't recognize, and they feel close to Darla. Like they hid behind her and kept me from seeing her," Ian said. "That's as close as I can come to describing it. Knowing they were there, I knew to look for them. But even knowing they're there, I can't quite get a fix on the third person."

He furrowed his brow, deep lines etching a groove between his eyes. "I don't understand."

"Neither do I," I said. "I've only just been learning that you're 'the Innkeeper' and the special powers that position gives you."

Ian waved a hand. "I'm still me. I don't even understand half the powers. And I guess that's normal. When the B&B chose me, the former Innkeeper, Blanche, was barely alive. No one really saw her except me. I guess you could say she was almost a ghost. Anyway, she could only teach me a little bit—every Innkeeper has slightly different powers. I guess that's like everyone else—She taught me some basic things I could do to learn more, but sometimes it's painful and hard, so I avoid doing too much, too quickly. That's probably bad."

Ian sighed and looked a bit defeated, as if he'd let people down.

"You're still you, remember?" I said. "I think the B&B knew who you were when it picked you. It probably even realized you'd avoid something that was too painful. Maybe it approved of that, because you weren't supposed to learn things fast, but at a rate you could absorb and understand."

Ian brightened a bit. "I'd like to think the place was that smart. Sometimes I'm not really certain. But you said a judgment?"

I nodded. "Do you know what that means?"

He shook his head. "I don't."

"I tried to ask more, but Tulip didn't respond and she went back to being a cat." I wished I had more information to give him.

Ian sighed. "I hate what's going on and I don't feel like I have the ability to handle it. But I guess, according to the cats, that's part of my job. I just always thought my job was welcoming people, not making sure everyone who was here was supposed to be here or rooting out felons for Xavier."

"It doesn't seem like it's your job to make sure they're supposed to be here, but just to know? And if someone is using magic, then that's harder. If our invisible person managed to murder Alexander Milton they're majorly powerful," I said. "Even if you'd done everything right on time, you might not have known everything."

"You're sweet to say that, but it's not exactly how the island thinks. Not if Tulip told you I would be judged. Or maybe she was warning me." Ian rolled his eyes and looked up at the ceiling.

He settled in and got silent for a moment. I felt a light tingle on my arms, but nothing like before. It didn't take long before Ian opened his eyes.

"I asked the B&B if I was in trouble and it said no. I could have done better, but they aren't angry with me or anything," Ian said. "It said a judgment is like a report card, but it's not like I've got a failing grade, more like I got a note on there that said 'Doesn't do this well, practice.'"

Trying to make light, I said, "It sounds more like disappointment that you aren't living up to your potential."

Ian looked crushed.

"What?" I asked.

"That's what my parents always said. If I weren't so into movies and gossip, I'd do better in school and stuff like that. They said I was wasting my potential," Ian said.

"Then I take it back. You're absolutely perfect." I gave him a long look, but Ian didn't seem to feel any better.

"It's okay to not be perfect," I said. "I mean if we were, we wouldn't have magic."

Ian laughed at that. "Right you are. I shouldn't sulk, but it's an old wound, you know?"

"And I'm sorry I touched it." I hoped that was enough. "You know you're my favorite person here on the island."

"Me and Bernice right?"

I laughed, but then sobered. "I actually like Bernice a bit. I mean I always know where I stand and exactly what she thinks. That's important."

"Is there anything else the magic said that might be important?" Ian asked. "I'm still worried about the person I can't sense. If you talk to Tulip or Peony again, see if they'll tell you who it is. Or even make sure it's a person and not, say, a spirit that followed someone here?"

"Could it be Alexander Milton?" I asked.

"I don't have a clue. But if it was, then he'd be on our side, don't you think? He wouldn't want someone terrorizing you. That's the sort of person he put away on Far Haven."

I had to agree.

"But now I'm hungry," Ian said. "I mean not really hungry, like I just did a ton of spells hungry, but I could eat. If we don't have any more secretive things to say, let's head to Derry's."

I got up to follow him through the door. A shadow moved just as the door opened. I frowned looking around. Ian didn't appear to see it. I hadn't been sure it was human, but something had been there. I hoped it wasn't something that shouldn't have been listening in.

Chapter Seventeen

Lunch with Ian was nice and we talked of inconsequential things. There are only so many times one can go over information before it starts becoming dull. Ian hates dull with a passion. I did notice, however, that he seemed ever so slightly distracted while we talked and ate. He was still concerned about what I had told him.

That afternoon, back in the office, I managed to get a little work done. Not nearly as much as I'd have liked, but more than I'd been doing the last couple of days. I counted that as a win. When it was time to head home, I detoured to the grocery store to pick up something for dinner. The air was pleasant, the dragon-flies flitted around, and I had a nice time chatting with acquaintances.

Naturally, there were rumors about Alexander Milton dying. I listened but didn't offer too much. I didn't want people to think I actually knew anything when I didn't. A couple of people asked me about Darla, but they were general inquiries. No one had seen her since she appeared in my office and at the library.

I did file away one little tidbit. Someone suggested

Darla could be hiding in the cave where Damien had performed his sacrifices. I knew exactly where the cave was as I'd been there. Peony had led me through underground tunnels and caverns to the cave where I'd burned the remains of a murdered woman, breaking the link Damien had to the island.

The cave would be a good place to hide. People didn't just go there.

I fixed myself some dinner, eating at the little dining room table, a small grayish brown and white thing that I'd found online—though on the island, I wasn't certain if anything was just *found*. The table fit the room perfectly, particularly with the matching chairs that had sky blue upholstery which I had fallen in love with.

I turned off the lights inside and turned on the outside light to watch the dragon-flies dancing around in swirls and circles. When they noticed me watching and eating, they flew closer and closer to the glass. A few landed on the glass and stayed there, though I had no idea how they found purchase. Of course, bugs sometimes did the same.

Peony and Tulip pawed at the glass trying to get at the little creatures, but the dragon-flies remained on the glass. One flew down and looked at Peony as she pawed at it. It breathed a thread of fire.

I watched as Peony's paw went through the glass to attempt to swat at the dragon-fly. I gasped, making Tulip give me a disgusted look.

Seconds later, Peony's paw was back inside, the dragon-fly was fluttering around slightly further from the glass, and the glass on my door was perfectly intact.

"You guys," I said. "I can't believe you can do that."

The dragon-fly that had been outside appeared above my head and flitted around, enjoying frustrating the cats as they made little squeaking noises, annoyed that they couldn't get to their prey.

Tulip leaped on my little dining room table. The Siamese stood in the middle and sat back on her hind legs, pawing at the dragon-fly. When she lost her balance she nearly fell on my dinner plate, but I moved it fast enough to avoid a collision.

"Get off the table!" I shouted.

Tulip leaped down.

The dragon-fly flitted in front of my face, looking at me. Its ears were as flat as Tulip's and its little tail hung down instead of floating out behind its back. Then it disappeared and was outside in the light, dancing around with its other friends.

Peony gave me a glare and went back to running her paws up and down the glass on the door.

I rolled my eyes. Dragon-flies were apparently not unlike cats. I finished my meal and took my plate over to the sink to put it and the pans I'd used in the dishwasher. I'd barely finished that chore when my phone rang.

I hurried over to get it. The way my life had been going, for all I knew the office could have burned down. I breathed a sigh of relief. Lauren. I hoped she had information.

"Darla's here," Lauren hissed. "I'm hiding in the library closet. She's looking for you."

I heard the sound of a door opening and then a thud. I heard several thumps and thuds before the phone hung up.

Automatically, I dialed 911 and got, of all people, Rose. I explained what was going on. She said she'd send someone. I hoped they got there in time. I liked Lauren and didn't want her injured. I should have called Xavier directly, though I didn't have his number. I resolved to add that to my phone as soon as I saw him, or maybe as soon as I saw Rose.

I paced around my house, heart thudding. I wanted to run over to the library, but knew I wouldn't be a match for anyone who had managed to harm Lauren.

I nearly jumped out of my skin when the doorbell rang. The only way I got myself to open the door was by reminding myself that Darla and whoever she was working with had never rung the bell before. It had to be someone I could trust. Besides, I had a peep hole.

Creeping slowly across the room, I inched towards the door. My hands were sweating. I pressed my eye to the peep hole. Nothing was there. I sent out a tendril of magic, but, again, I found nothing. No human stood on my porch.

My hands began to sweat. I backed up a half-step, trying to decide what to do. Peony meowed at me and this time I did jump. If cats could roll their eyes, she would have.

I took that as a sign that it was okay to open the door. My hands fumbled with the latch and at first I couldn't quite get a grip. Finally, though, I was able to press down on the front door latch and open the door.

No one stood on my front porch. About three dozen dragon-flies were flitting around the yard, moving quickly the way they did when they were anxious. I closed the door, wondering if they'd scared someone off. If so, I mentally thanked them. But I was still puzzled by what was going on. I hated that whatever it was seemed to be focused on me.

Chapter Eighteen

I debated calling the police on the non-emergency number, but I didn't know what Rose would do. Xavier was, hopefully, at the library. I tried calling Lauren again, but unsurprisingly, my call went to her voicemail. I paced around the house.

Peony and Tulip watched me.

If Lauren was hurt, she'd go to the clinic and they'd work with her there. I called over there because someone is always on. Rebecca, the night nurse, answered and said that Dr. Mulrooney was in with Lauren just then. While she was unconscious and had some bruises, she was stable.

I hung up in case Dr. Mulrooney needed Rebecca's assistance. Of course, in those kinds of emergencies, Cassandra usually helped out. That allowed Rebecca to man the front desk, which was always covered.

The call made me feel a little better. Still, while I'd had a nice evening, even the nicest day I'd had since they'd found the body, whatever relaxation I had acquired was gone in a heartbeat and I was back to being agitated.

I tried to make a list of the things I wanted to know,

but I couldn't even focus on that. Peony came up to me and started purring. While I knew she meant to calm me, it wasn't helpful. Tulip jumped up and sat beside me and added her purrs to Peony's. Even then, I couldn't sit still.

Running down to the cave where Ann Rogers's body had been stored *seemed* like a great idea. In theory.

As much as I wanted to, even I was not foolish enough to actually go down there. Alone. At night.

Still, it was like the very idea had put a compulsion on me. I had to force myself to stay in my house and let the police take care of things.

My feet tapped out tunes on the floor and I had just settled in to sit on my hands, hoping that would make it harder for me to stand up, when someone banged on the door.

Peony raised her head and then leaped off and went running towards the door. Tulip remained in place on the sofa and looked annoyed. I figured that if even one of the cats was eager to see who it was, I was probably safe. I did look out the peep hole just to be sure. Xavier waited on the porch.

I opened the door and let him in. He was alone.

"I left Carl at the library trying to put together what happened," Xavier said after the initial niceties had been observed, truncated though they were.

"Is Lauren going to be okay? I talked to Rebecca and she said she was stable." I wanted reassurance that Lauren would be fine. I didn't quite know why she was targeted along with me. I didn't think it was because we were friends. We were friendly, mostly because of her work. But she wasn't my closest friend here.

Xavier sighed. "I think so. It looks like it was a powerful sleep spell. She hit her head when she fell. Dr. Mulrooney was able to wake her, briefly, but she fell back under almost immediately. Lauren told us that Darla showed up at the library. You said she called and told you Darla was looking for you?"

"She did. I don't know why she didn't call you first. She said she was hiding in a closet." I rubbed my arms. We were sitting at opposite ends of my sofa, where Xavier had led us while doing the initial hellos.

"That's where we found her, or rather partly in and partly out of the closet on the floor. She doesn't remember why she thought she needed to call you, but she remembers doing it."

"Could Darla have told her she'd leave her alone if she got me there?" I asked.

Xavier shrugged. "It seems like Darla is after you."

"Now it seems she's after Lauren, too," I added. "While I think of Lauren as a friend, she's not my closest friend. If it were about someone close to me, I'd expect Ian to have been targeted. Even Jack spends more time with me, although we're coworkers rather than friends. When I saw Darla in my office, Lauren saw her at the same time in the library."

Xavier looked thoughtful. "If this is about Damien, someone could think you two know something. Lauren's the librarian. She's never been shy about looking things up when she wants to know something. You were there when Damien was taken into custody. You talked to the ghost of the woman who was his first victim."

"If it's something I know, then I don't know what that something is. I've been learning some things online because there's so much about magic and the enclaves that I don't really understand yet."

"It takes time," Xavier said. "It took me a few years before I felt like had enough information to know what to do."

"I heard you worked at Far Haven." I just blurted that out. It didn't have anything to do with the conversation. I didn't think Xavier had anything to do with what was happening but if someone was after me, I needed to know as much as I could, even about things that might not be completely related.

"I did," Xavier said. "I'd come up there through Sweet Peach Enclave—which, if anyone asked me, was the stupidest name ever. They weren't even in Georgia but North Carolina. I had the magic to handle rogue mages and Far Haven needed someone. I trained under Alexander. His death is a huge loss."

"Could the fact that you're here be the reason he was dumped on Jewel? I mean, we've all thought about Damien and stuff, but maybe there was something about you?"

Xavier sighed. "I doubt it. There's no reason to think that I'd be more upset about Alexander than anyone else. He had closer connections elsewhere. Damien is the most likely thread and yes, I'm involved in that, too. I arrested him, remember."

He was right.

"I have figured out that someone put something in Alexander's coffee, probably shortly before he got on the ferry. It looks like someone used magic against him after the drugs had taken effect. Even if he tried to defend himself, he would have been sluggish and not thinking clearly. If they knew him well, they'd have known he wouldn't want to do anything too spectacular where ordinary folks might notice. The ferry was perfect."

"Oh!" I said, when Tulip leaped up and tapped me with her paw. She gave me a long look and then a loud Siamese yowl. I had the feeling I'd been ordered to say something.

"I don't know if Ian told you. Tulip told me there were three people on the island. So it's Darla, and two others. Ian kind of has a sense of one of the others but not the third." I hoped that's what the cat wanted.

Xavier raised an eyebrow. "That shouldn't be. The Innkeeper always knows who's here. Even the dragon-fly effect shouldn't make it harder for him to understand things. At least it hasn't before."

"That's what I've heard," I said. I didn't add anything about Tulip talking about judgment. I wondered if Xavier had ever heard of such a thing, but that comment felt private, though I couldn't have said why.

"None of this should be happening. We don't have any clues as to who would want to murder Alexander. No one else on Far Haven is missing. Damien is still in his cell and they've made sure the magical enhancements remain in place. No one can feel any magic in him, either. And he's aging. Quickly," Xavier said. He was clearly thinking out loud.

"It seems that it's related to something around Damien, though," I said. "How was it that he managed to find a way that would confer magic on him? I mean, did he read a book? And if so, why haven't other people read it?"

Xavier shook his head, his dark eyes troubled. "Those are questions I can't answer. It's the sort of thing I'd ask Lauren to look into and maybe that's why she's been targeted."

"We need to keep all avenues of investigation open," Xavier continued, "though I lean towards this having something to do with Damien and that Lauren was searching something that the people hiding didn't want us to find out too quickly. Lauren wasn't badly hurt. The sleep spell didn't do much damage, although it looks like the library put up quite a fight for her. There were books all over. Even with the mess, I'd think being attacked would just make Lauren more likely to go looking for information, so this has to be a delaying tactic. I'm just not sure why."

"We talked about whether someone like me, someone with spirit magic, could astral project and then possess another person," I said. "I know she was going to look into that because she thought the question was interesting."

Now, I was going to have to look into it myself. I hoped I my research skills were up to par.

Xavier rubbed his chin, eyes narrowed slightly. "Now that would be an interesting thing. How did you get onto that?"

"The other night, when Darla was at both my office and the library, at about the same time. Lauren and I wondered how that could be done. I wondered if maybe I'd seen a ghost or something. Darla didn't seem to want to attack me. She'd cry and then her face would change and she'd attack. The fact that she was in two places made me think about someone possessing her…" I trailed off unable to figure out how to say what I was thinking.

"You think that someone took over her body and perhaps took her to the library because they were worried about Lauren. What you saw was Darla's spirit, perhaps trying to fight off another spirit." Xavier summed up.

"Something like that. Or maybe someone was possessing her body and made it come here. Maybe Lauren saw Darla's astral projection, trying to warn her what was happening? Or maybe the library just felt safe to her?"

That made Xavier smile slightly. "Darla never found the library particularly comforting. In fact, I'm not sure she'd ever been there. Besides, I'm not at all certain that someone without spirit magic could see someone astral projecting."

"Maybe if the person who was projecting wanted them to?" I asked. Of course, ghosts might want more than just those of us with spirit magic to see them.

"It's a stretch," Xavier said. I knew that meant he didn't really agree.

"Everything seems to revolve around spirit magic, I'm glad that Bernice has called in Lucas Moore. He's an expert on spirit magic. I believe he'll be on the morning ferry tomorrow. I got a message that he had just missed the evening one. The U Council is on their way as well, though that takes longer to get everyone coordinated. I am not looking forward to them descending upon the island."

Xavier and I finished our conversation. I wasn't quite comfortable though. The fact that someone who could help had just missed a ferry and Lauren had been attacked made me think that there was something we shouldn't learn, at least not yet.

I wished I knew what it was.

<u>Chapter Nineteen</u>

To say I had a restless night would have been an under-statement. I didn't even try to get to bed until well after midnight. My mind couldn't have found a shut-off button if my life had depended on it. I'd done research on astral projection for mages but hadn't found anything that suggested that yes, I could possess someone if I knew how to do it, or worse, that a living mage could possess me. I'd always been under the impression that possession meant by a dead person. The idea of a living person taking over my body made me shudder even more.

Even when I finally crawled into bed and dozed, I was plagued with odd half-remembered dreams. I mean, Ian trying to serve bologna sandwiches on white bread for breakfast instead of Eggs Benedict and saying it was better didn't strike me as prophetic. Unless, of course, we were going into an egg shortage. Heaven knew that in the last few years we'd had enough shortages.

The morning dawned tired, damp, and gray. My body felt heavy and sluggish and I struggled to push myself to shower and get ready for work. My stomach had tied itself in knots of worry.

I wanted to call the clinic to find out how Lauren was doing, but my slow morning had put me so far behind I didn't even have time to make a cup of coffee.

Having magical cats seemed like it would be more useful if said cats would make coffee first thing in the morning when I was dragging. But then again, I had cats not dogs. There were magical dogs on the island, too. Perhaps they were kinder to their people.

Outside, the gray, overcast day smelled like rain, but my house hadn't offered umbrellas, so it wasn't likely to start in the next few minutes. Dragon-flies surrounded me as soon as I came out. Instead of following me like soldiers in a parade, these swarmed around me like midges in a swamp. I even had to wave my hand in front of my face a few times so that I could keep walking.

The discordant sound of waves crashing against the island without any symmetry surrounded me much like the dragon-flies. The sound was every bit as irritating. I felt as if I were out of step with the entire world and nothing was going to make me happy, except maybe a solution to the mystery and a really long nap.

Jack wasn't at the office when I got there. While fishing for my key, the rain started. There's a cover over the porch and while I didn't get wet, it was one more annoyance in a line of many. The dragon-flies didn't seem bothered by the falling rain and continued to hover around me, their wings nearly silent against the noises of the island.

Finally, I got the door opened and slipped inside. A dozen or so of the dragon-flies flew in with me, while the rest appeared to fly around the sides of the office, about half the remaining dragon-flies to one side and the second half to the other. It wasn't their usual formation.

I didn't let the dozen that were inside worry me. Inside the quiet office, their wings made a low hum. I hung up my jacket and went to the kitchen to make coffee. I pulled out my favorite pod flavor and filled a mug with water. The water made a hissing sound coming from the faucet. Normally, our water sounds like water. This sounded like there was something wrong with the pipe.

A red dragon-fly drive-bombed the sink, splashing in the stream that came from the faucet. I pulled my mug back and watched while it hovered there like it was taking a shower. A particularly long shower. A headache began to form behind my eyes. I rubbed my temple, still waiting.

I turned off the water. The dragon-fly flew off. As soon as I turned it back on, the same hiss coming through the faucet, another dragon-fly, this one green, hovered under it.

"If you wanted to get wet, all you had to do was stay outside," I muttered.

The little dragon blew a thread of fire at me.

As there were other little dragons swarming around, I left the kitchen. Most followed me, but I noticed several stayed fluttering around the kitchen. One seemed very interested in the coffee pod. I yawned. I needed caffeine.

Instead of going to my office, I grabbed my jacket to walk down to the grocery store. The deli would have fresh coffee and maybe the dragon-flies would let me get some from there. I grabbed an umbrella from the urn by the door and headed out. I waved at Gretchen who was hurrying back up the hill having purchased a sack of groceries for her day.

"I heard about Lauren," Gretchen said quietly. "It's just terrible. Are you doing okay? No one came to hurt you last night?"

"No," I said. "So far, I've been okay. I haven't seen Darla at all."

Gretchen touched my arm, her eye serious as she looked at me. I felt warmth going through me, relaxing me but also helping my energy. "Be safe."

Then she was gone. Oddly, I felt safer. My arms hadn't tingled at all but perhaps it was just knowing that someone cared about that me that did it. I hurried down the street to get coffee. The deli made a decent cup. I hated to spend money on something I could easily serve myself in the morning, but apparently, I wasn't supposed to make my own.

Three dragon flies hovered around the door to the grocery store when I went in. None followed me through the door. None popped in as I ordered my single cup, a large one. No matter what Gretchen had done, I was still tired and I needed to be awake to think clearly. Not that I expected I'd get much done that day. Still, if whoever had been in the library showed up in the office, I wanted to be more awake and less sluggish.

The three little dragon-flies flew around me as I walked back to the office. None of them seemed interested in my coffee. The others that had followed me to work still flew around the building. It seemed like the entire swarm came out to check on what I was doing when I got back. I shook my head.

Then I slipped inside to get started on my day. Jack still wasn't in the office, which was unusual. I considered calling him but decided I'd give him a bit more time. We weren't busy and he didn't work on a time-clock. It was just strange for him. He hadn't mentioned anything going on that would keep him out of the office for the morning or even the whole day.

After half an hour, when he still hadn't come in, I gave

him a call. Jack didn't answer his phone. I double checked that I had the correct number. I did. I considered calling again, but decided against it. If he wasn't answering, he wasn't answering. I hadn't heard that the dragon-fly effect would interfere with normal phone service. I was told they only messed with magical spells, from people, not buildings, as Ian said.

Now, I worried about Jack. I bit my lip wondering if I should call Xavier. I could go over to Jack's home and check on him but I didn't know where he lived. I mean, I had a general idea but I'd never been there. Ian would know. Maybe Ian's powers would even be able to ascertain if Jack needed help. He'd at least know Jack was alive and well and on the island.

I finished the coffee I'd gotten at the deli. I set the mug aside to return it when I went back and then headed over to the B&B. The rain had stopped, though the day remained overcast. The umbrella urn had disappeared, so I figured it was safe enough to walk.

This time, I had all the dragon-flies following me. Some flew in front, like they were leading me. Others flew around me like little escorts but the vast majority of them followed me as I walked across the street and slightly up the hill.

The pink and green Victorian B&B blended into the gray clouds that hung low in the sky. A chill breeze hit me just as I walked into the garden. Three cats, one black, one orange, and one white sat under the little Japanese maple that was starting to leaf out again now that it was spring. They watched me.

The black one crouched down, his tail twitching. He stared at one of the dragon-flies, ready to pounce. One of them, perhaps the one that the black cat watched, spit a thread of fire at the cats. It reminded me a child sticking its tongue out at another child who wanted to fight.

I rolled my eyes as I climbed the stairs to the B&B. The dragon-flies swarmed up over the porch and fluttered around, several of them shooting out little threads of flame or puffing out a bit of smoke from their mouths, always in the direction of the cats.

Ian was in the dining room, wiping down tables. It looked like the breakfast crowd had gone.

"I finished breakfast already," he said, looking apologetic. "I could have the cook whip you up something?"

"I'm not here for food." Naturally, my stomach growled just then. "Really." I added.

Ian looked skeptical.

"Really," I repeated. "Jack didn't come into the office. I was wondering if you knew if he was okay."

Ian half-closed his eyes and took a deep breath.

"I can't tell if people are okay, but someone left the island this morning and when I focused, I knew it was Jack," he said a few moments later.

"He left the island?" I asked. "He said nothing to me. It's not like he can't take a vacation, but it'd have been nice if he said something! You haven't heard that he's had a family emergency or something have you?"

Ian shook his head. He leaned against the table and watched me. "You don't think that this is about Darla and the mysterious people on the island, do you?"

"That's why I was worried. I mean, Lauren was attacked. Xavier thinks it's because she might have been researching a thread someone didn't want her to get to just yet, but maybe it was because someone saw her having dinner with me?" I said. "And then Jack…"

"Works with you," Ian finished. "Although I doubt anyone would mistake you two for bosom buddies. Jack isn't anyone's dear friend. He's nice, but he's obsessive and not all that interested in people."

"I don't know. The last couple of day he's said some stuff that makes me think he's far more astute than he lets on." I repeated a few of the things Jack had said that seemed quite on point. I avoided anything that might embarrass Ian though.

"That's not the Jack I know," Ian said. He pushed off the table and flicked the towel he'd been using to wipe the table.

A tingle went up my arms and a moment later all the tables were clean, the chairs tucked in and everything looked ready for the light dinner that the B&B would serve.

"But did you know him? It's not like he's outgoing, as you said."

"I knew Brent for about a month after I got here. Back then, the accounting office had two bookkeepers and an accountant," Ian said. "Anyway, Brent worked with Jack for some time but he thought Jack was naïve in how he viewed people. Jack might have been nice, but he had no real insight into who other people were or why they did what they did. Jack comes in for dinner sometimes, not a lot. I think he prefers to make his own food to his own specifications, but tax time and all…" Ian raised his hands and shrugged.

"Anyway, when he comes in and I try to talk to him or whatever, the things he says do seem naïve and not nearly as astute as the observations he made to you." Ian's eyes hardened and he looked expectant, as if there was something there I should get.

Then it hit me. "Almost like he was possessed," I whispered.

Ian raised an eyebrow and nodded.

"But he doesn't have spirit magic, so that can't be it," I protested, but it was weak.

"Maybe there's something we don't know," Ian said, equally quiet.

I knew there was plenty I didn't know. I just didn't know how that lack worked into this situation. I wondered if I would ever stop feeling so inadequate.

Chapter Twenty

Ian insisted I call Xavier, which I did. Naturally, I got Rose. She said she'd let him know and he'd get back to me. It sounded as if there were other things going on at the station.

"Well, given that your stomach was talking, I'll go fix you something to eat," Ian said already turning to head back to the kitchen.

I smelled the lingering scents of bacon and his delicious coffee.

"My stomach might think it needs food, but honestly, I am not all that hungry," I said. "Too nervous."

"I'll just fix up a little toast and maybe some more coffee," Ian said.

I settled at a little two-top dining room table near the rounded window of the dining room. There weren't many tables that morning. On busy mornings, the B&B expanded the place so that more people could be seated for breakfast at one time. I'd never asked Ian but I wondered how that worked for making and serving the food. So far as

I knew, magic couldn't clone someone. Perhaps that was a question worth asking.

In no time, he sashayed out with a tray that included toast, coffee and an assortment of sweet breakfast treats including a mixed berry scone that I was partial to.

Ian set everything down and poured coffee into two mugs. It smelled divine. I nibbled at a slice of toast, though my eyes remained on the scones.

"For someone who wasn't hungry, you're eyeing those scones like you're a hawk and they're a particularly juicy-looking rabbit," Ian said, taking a sip of his coffee. He set the cup down and waited.

"They do look good," I said. "I was thinking, though. How does it work for cooking and serving when the dining room expands? How do you keep up?"

Ian laughed. "So not the question I was expecting." He went silent and looked around. "Asher, my main cook, just works harder. We can magically cook some things, too. It was easier with Darla because she's young and she and I could make sure we were both moving fast and efficiently. I have a spell for that. It's harder with Edie because she's older and can't physically move all that fast any more. I really need someone else to work here."

"So the B&B doesn't mysteriously create a clone of your cook?" I pressed.

"Ah!" Ian nodded. "I see where you're going with this. No. I can't clone people and so far as I know, neither can the island. It's something about life. We can make things, even food that nourishes, but we can't breathe life into something. Well…"

"Well what?" I asked, swallowing another bite of toast, this one slightly larger. Ian was staring out the window.

"Well, it occurred to me that you deal with spirit magic

and ghosts so maybe it would be possible for someone with spirit magic to create life," Ian said.

I finished my toast and thought about what he'd said.

"Darla," I finally said.

Ian shook his head, frowning. "She's not that good. But I bet soon enough you'll be able to ask. Your expert on spirit magic arrived on the early morning ferry that Jack left on."

"Is he here?" I asked, meaning the B&B. The way I craned my neck to look around left Ian in no doubt what I meant.

"Nope. Bernice met him at the dock. I think he's at the police station. Probably talking to Xavier and they're probably talking about how Jack disappeared and was acting oddly. He'll have an opinion on whether Jack was possessed or not based on the information Rose gives him."

"If he waits that long," I said. Rose did not move fast.

Grinning, Ian grabbed one of the gooey looking sweet rolls and took a huge bite. "Rose moves faster than anyone gives her credit for. Don't underestimate her."

"It seems like they'd want to talk to me directly…" I trailed off as I heard someone on the front porch. The dragon-flies started making their tiny peeps as the door opened.

Ian stood up and looked through the main door.

"Bernice," he said. "And Xavier. And you must be Lucas."

I stood as well, setting aside the scone that had a single bite taken from it. It was probably good that I did stand because the little two top table I'd been at morphed into a round five seater. Somehow, my plate and coffee remained in place.

Bernice led the way into the dining room. She nodded

at me. "I looked in at the accounting office but the door was locked?"

"Jack didn't come in this morning," I said. "I talked to Ian and we called the police."

Xavier came in while I was talking. "Rose let me know. I figured I was already on my way here. You said Ian thought he had left this morning?"

I nodded. "It could have been innocent—you know that he forgot to say—but he'd been acting unlike himself for a few days. Very perceptive on how people would think. He was actually very nice."

"Is he not normally nice?" Lucas asked. The best word to describe him would have been round. His face was round, his body was slightly round. His eyes were the roundest eyes I had ever seen and a startling shade of green. The short trim of his blonde hair, probably bleached, considering how pale it was, made his head look even rounder than it should have.

"He's quiet," I said. "Rather obsessive. Stays to himself."

"He's not a people person," Ian added. "He's often been naïve about people's motivations and why they react the way they do."

Bernice agreed. "Jack was many things, but insightful was not one of them."

Lucas looked thoughtful. He spied the food on the table and settled in at a seat. Bernice followed and then Xavier. Ian sashayed off to get more coffee and more pastries. I went back to picking at my scone. I loved them, but my stomach was in knots.

"The dragon-flies are worried about you," Lucas said looking at me. He grabbed the other scone, the same mixed berry flavor. "They told me that before I walked in.

In fact, I think they're standing guard. Against spirits or a spirit. They were somewhat confused about that."

"Did they say why the spirit is dangerous to me?" I asked. I mean I could ask them myself, later, but if Lucas had suffered the chill I got from speaking to them, no need for me to go through it. Besides, I had my suspicions. The dragon-flies might pick that up and give me the answer I was looking for.

"They are aware that this spirit holds ill-will towards you and has since it became spirit," Lucas said. "Did you kill someone?"

I hesitated.

Bernice jumped in. "No. She reflected magic that was about to destroy her back to the one who threw it at her."

"Here?" Lucas seemed surprised.

"Reflected magic," Xavier said. "If someone means another harm and that magic is reflected back, they aren't safe."

Lucas cocked his head, almost as if he'd never heard of such a thing, though everyone on the island had acted as if someone dying from not being able to catch magic reflected back to them was a known thing.

"Damien was stopped and arrested just after you arrived as well." Lucas finally spoke. He seemed to be putting the pieces together.

"Sharon," Ian said sadly.

I agreed with his sorrow. Sharon had seemed like a wonderful woman. I had liked her. She'd been welcoming and warm and kind. Until she wasn't. Then she'd been intent upon murdering me to keep me from stopping Damien. She wanted immortality and was determined to have it. It appeared that death hadn't changed her.

"I will meditate on her," Lucas said. He finished the scone, stood up, and looked around.

Everyone else remained seated. Even Ian didn't seem certain about what to do, so he waited.

Lucas headed out the door of the dining room. I had no doubt the B&B would create the perfect room for him to meditate in.

"I don't like that Jack just left," Xavier said in a low voice. "Who knows if the people with Darla left, too?"

"They're still here," Ian said in a low voice. "Now that I know they're here, at least two of them, I can feel them. It's still foggy, but I definitely have a sense that they're here."

Bernice breathed out. "I feel like having Lucas here is a piece that we've needed."

"Do we know any more about what happened to Alexander or why someone would want to murder him?" I asked.

Xavier shook his head. "Far Haven is investigating on their end. They're looking through personal effects and calls that came in to him to see if there's a clue there. He was fine when he left. Damien shows no sign of magic, and because of that, Alexander wasn't even assigned to watch his wing."

I pushed down a shudder at the thought of a wing full of magical criminals. Despite having run into Damien first thing, I tended to trust other mages. There was something authentic about the people I had met here. And yet, someone had tried to hurt Lauren.

"I forgot, with everything going on with Jack," I said. "How is Lauren?"

"She's still in the hospital and she's fallen back to sleep. Dr. Mulrooney doesn't have an explanation for it. Most likely it's the dragon-fly effect. Unfortunately, that means we can't question her about what was going on. Dr. Mulrooney didn't want to bother her last night and none of us thought she wouldn't be able to answer questions today. Maybe later." Xavier trailed off, clearly frustrated with the turn of events.

"How did the island let that happen?" I asked. "Someone could have killed her. We're supposed to be safe here."

"That's probably why she didn't die," Ian said. "The island doesn't prevent accidents or harm. It just makes sure we don't die. I wasn't that worried about Lauren for that very reason. And besides, I went up to the library and I saw the mess. The books put up a good fight."

I pictured the library books flying at a potential murderer, their pages flapping, perhaps opening and closing their covers trying to keep the librarian safe. It was amusing on one hand but also frightening on the other. What if the books took a dislike to someone? Or did books care so long as the librarian was safe?

"I don't understand why she called me rather than the police." I frowned. The scone I'd eaten felt as if it stuck in my throat. I hated that she risked her life to call me and not the police.

"It is something I've wondered about myself," Bernice said. "Did you actually hear Lauren or did you hear someone sounding like Lauren. Did you consider going over there?"

I nodded. I had. But I wasn't stupid either. I also suspected that Peony and Tulip wouldn't have let me go.

"They could have wanted to draw you there," Bernice said.

"They couldn't have murdered me, though," I said. "Even without the dragon-flies the island protects me, right?"

"It won't protect you from being taken off the island and onto a ferry," Xavier said. "And the island's idea of what is safe is different from that of a human. Someone could have kept you drugged or unconscious overnight and then brought you on the ferry this morning. If Jack was possessed or charmed, maybe he was supposed to take you with him. He could even have been told to leave and find you on the ferry to kill you."

I swallowed hard as a chill went through me.

Lucas walked in then, looking grave.

Bernice looked up, expectant. Lucas slumped in the chair and put his head down. We all looked at each other, waiting.

Chapter Twenty-One

Ian got up and went back to the kitchen. I had no doubt he'd be making the tea he often made when someone had overused their powers. I doubted that was exactly what had happened with Lucas, but such a brew couldn't hurt.

Such silence descended upon the B&B that the tiny sounds Ian made in the kitchen, pulling down a mug and filling it with hot water, seemed loud in the dining room. Xavier cleared his throat once, startling me just a bit.

Lucas, remained slumped in the chair, eyes closed.

Bernice sat equally silent, though she wasn't slumped. I wasn't sure it was possible for Bernice to slump. Sitting upright and at attention, she waited without a single fidget. Xavier, at least, gave in to the human need to move a bit here and there and he seemed relieved when Ian returned with a mug of tea smelling of cloves and cinnamon.

"Drink up," Ian said to Lucas. He knelt down in front of him and helped him bring the cup to his lips.

Lucas took the mug, clearly not as exhausted as he looked and sipped. Even then he didn't open his eyes.

Ian stood and backed up. He looked puzzled by Lucas's response. Normally, people either required more help or they were able to open their eyes when they could hold a mug.

Lucas took a bigger sip this time and then drew in a breath. Finally, he opened his eyes and leaned forward, elbows on the table. He let his head drop dramatically.

Part of me was curious as to what could have happened. Another part of me wanted to roll my eyes. I wondered if he always did that. If so, I couldn't help but wonder if he was as good with spirits as they said. I much preferred Bernice's silent stillness, no matter how awkward it could feel when I couldn't quite keep up.

"Well?" Xavier said breaking the silence.

"The ghost is named Sharon," Lucas said. He looked around to see if anyone was surprised by that. If he were expecting gasps he got none. While we hadn't been certain, we had hypothesized such a thing.

"She's the one possessing Darla. Darla opened herself to her. I felt traces of a male that Sharon was close to. Powerful, though he's gone now. I take it that was Damien?" Lucas looked around at us.

Bernice gave a single dip of her chin, which satisfied Lucas.

"I thought so, though her spirit was cagey about who it was. There's another spirit here, but I couldn't get a fix on him. Someone spelled him to keep him quiet, but he's too powerful. I expect, because his body landed here, that it could be Alexander. I've met him a handful of times and it feels like him. There's someone else, but I can't get a fix," Lucas added.

"There are two other people here hidden by magic, too," Ian said. "I couldn't feel them until I was made aware that they were there. The more I focus, I get the sense that one is a woman, though I can't quite be sure. It's like trying to catch a shadow."

"Sharon wasn't talkative. She's been able to possess Darla to get things done. I asked how Darla came to be here but Sharon clammed up. She knows but isn't willing to talk," Lucas said. "And Alexander can't talk."

"Did they appear?" I asked. I had felt no tingling on my arms, no chill. Usually I was aware when spirits were around.

Lucas shook his head. "My talent doesn't work like that. I can hear them. More like a medium in a séance, though I have heard you can see them as well as talk to them?"

I nodded.

"That's an unusual gift. The dragon-flies tell me you're quite powerful if untrained. They struggle to communicate with you because you get so cold. I can teach you to remain warm, though."

That would be a helpful thing to know.

"Is Sharon trying to possess Holly in order to access her powers?" Xavier asked.

"I don't know. I didn't think to ask that. Even if that was her plan, I doubt she'd have told me. I can infer certain things, rather like a psychic, but if they really don't want me to know, a spirit can hide things. Holly might be different. I suspect that she's more in-tune with them. Did I hear that one may have tried to possess you already, but the dragon-flies interfered?"

I told Lucas about seeing Darla and the headache after.

"It was probably Sharon and you fought her off." Lucas seemed to think that was a good thing. "She's not the most powerful spirit out there, but she is determined.

Fortunately, most spirits don't mean us harm. At worst they want to talk your ear off."

At least I had done something right.

"Is there anything else you can tell us?" Bernice asked.

"My impression is that Sharon wants to sacrifice Holly in the way that Damien sacrificed the other women. She believes that will allow her to influence the island from the other side, so to speak. She also hopes that doing so will re-link the island to Damien and he'll be able to escape Far Haven," Lucas said. "I think she's wrong. Especially with Alexander's spirit hanging around."

I couldn't image how they'd expect to sacrifice me. The island would keep me from being killed. But if my body was possessed, would the island still recognize me? I didn't dare speak the thought out loud.

"He was coming here for a reason," Xavier said. "I wish they'd tell us why that was."

"I heard that Darla was attacked before coming here, too, possibly being driven here. I had a thought that Alexander wasn't able to be possessed and so they overdosed him. Darla was able to be possessed, so they let her live," Lucas said.

"But we have at least two other live people here," Ian said. "Or possibly one plus a spirit."

Lucas frowned. "I don't believe I sensed any non-resident spirits other than Alexander. Are you sure that's not the third person you can't quite focus on?"

Ian shook his head. "I wasn't able to sense them at all. It's only because the island communicated that there were three outsiders here that I became aware of them. It didn't seem like one was Alexander."

"I didn't get that impression either," I said.

Lucas didn't like that. That was a piece of the puzzle he didn't understand. I wondered if it could be someone else possessed. Perhaps there was another missing person from one of the enclaves. I said as much. Bernice rose to go make some calls.

Lucas ate a sweet roll from the basket of treats Ian had brought out. He chewed thoughtfully and then licked his fingers.

"I miss having breakfast at the B&B when I travel. I had to stay at a hotel in Michigan this morning and their continental breakfast just wasn't quite the same."

Ian smiled a little, but didn't offer to make a full breakfast, which surprised me. Usually, he leaped to be of service, like when he'd gotten the tea. He rubbed the side of his head lightly.

"Headache?" I asked quietly.

Ian met my eyes and then gave a single nod.

Xavier frowned. "Do you get headaches?"

"Not often," Ian said.

Lucas sat up straight, putting down the sweet roll. He took my hand. His was dry and colder than I expected. I thought that my hands felt chilly often, but his were like ice.

"Focus," he ordered. This wasn't the slightly quiet, perhaps bumbling man who was more interested in eating than in the mystery of what was happening on the island. This was the man who had proved himself to be an expert.

I focused on my breathing as Bernice had taught me. I felt my power being fed to Lucas. Normally I just felt someone working magic, the tingle on my arms and then after, I'd feel weak. At least that's how it had been when Bernice worked with me to teach me how to share my power with another. This time I felt something inside me, like water, flowing away from me. I had a sense that I could stop it if I wanted, but I was entranced by the mental images I saw in my mind's eye.

Sharon's spirt hovered over Ian. She kept trying to open the top of his skull, but I saw a feline shadow, Ian's cat, Socrates, perhaps, closing the skull before she could get in.

"Be gone," Lucas said. Or maybe he thought it. I knew the voice came from him, but like the dragon-fly's voice it didn't seem to have an origin.

Sharon paused and stared at us. Her image started to dissolve slowly, but she held onto Ian. I saw the magic being leached from him. The slight smile on her face suggested that was actually her goal all along.

An image of Lucas, sort of shimmery and gold leaped into the picture and pushed her away. Once Sharon wasn't touching Ian, Ian, who wasn't exactly Ian but a caricature of himself, grabbed at her and began to suck the power back into his body. I watched it all as if I were sitting in a theater watching a film, still feeling Lucas's very cold hand in mine. It twitched now and then.

Ian disappeared from my mind's eye. Hopefully, that meant he was okay. Sharon remained, looking somewhat depleted. Lucas pointed a finger at her and she pointed back. I didn't see any magic running between them, but they swayed and leaned as if they saw and felt something.

Lucas and Sharon continued to battle until finally her image disappeared. I smelled something slightly damp and rotten and then there was only darkness behind my eyes.

I didn't open my eyes right then. I waited for Lucas to tell me to. I didn't feel my magic being drained any longer. I realized that it had been a few minutes or perhaps only seconds since I had noticed the draining.

Lucas dropped my hand.

I opened my eyes.

Ian sat there, frowning. Xavier watched carefully.

I breathed in. Only then did I realize I had been

holding my breath for who knew how long. I felt dizzy. Black fuzzy lines began to encroach on my vision. I put a hand out on the table as I leaned forward.

The last thing I saw was Ian getting up, probably to get me some tea.

<u>Chapter Twenty-Two</u>

Hot spicy water dribbled down my throat, almost choking me. I coughed and sputtered. Realized I wasn't quite awake. I still felt dizzy as I sat up and opened my eyes. Ian was beside me, holding a mug that smelled of his typical restorative tea.

"Drink," he said, pushing the tea towards my mouth.

I couldn't refuse. I took the mug, though his hands helped me steady it. I felt strong enough to hold it although I worried that I might faint again. I couldn't remember fainting before. Normally, I just sort of slumped down. The dizziness was a new thing.

Lucas and Xavier were talking in low voices, but I wasn't yet awake enough to understand the words or even if they were talking about me.

I sipped at the tea at first. It wasn't too hot. I knew it would the right temperature in the same way I knew the B&B expanded and contracted to fit the needs of the island. At the same time, I had years of experience of having to sip a hot drink before taking a bigger drink.

Once I'd assured myself that I could drink the tea, I gulped down a larger mouthful and then leaned back.

The world was coming back into focus. Bernice was still in the other room making calls, so I hadn't been out for too awfully long.

Lucas noticed me looking around, sitting upright. He pushed the basket of treats towards me. I grabbed the last berry scone and took a bite. Few things were more heavenly. The sugar on the top was exactly what my body craved. The tart and sweet flavor of the berries melted on my tongue.

"Better?" Lucas asked.

I swallowed before saying I was. "I've not fainted before," I added, somewhat embarrassed, as if doing so made me weak or something.

"It happens," Lucas said. "You watched me. I could feel you. I had a lot of your magic, so you definitely extended yourself, possibly overextended yourself, but I can see why you were so interesting to Damien. You have a lot of power. You're pretty much untrained when it comes to spirit. If you knew how to order spirits the way I do, Sharon would have vanished in an instant. I think the only reason she noticed me was because I was using your power."

"Next time we do a training, could you not overwork Holly?" Ian asked. "Her power isn't unlimited and this time she fainted."

Lucas gave a tight smile. It stretched his mouth out almost from edge to edge of his round face.

"That wasn't my intention," Lucas said quietly. He, too, was drinking more of Ian's restorative tea. One of Ian's natural powers was the ability to help someone heal. It didn't depend upon the B&B, although the fact that he could heal and help people feel more rested probably made him more desirable to the B&B when it needed a new Innkeeper. Fortunately, the tea hadn't been subject to the dragon-fly effect, at least not that I had noticed. Perhaps later I'd be wired.

Ian sighed and peered into the basket of goodies. He rolled his eyes and sashayed off to the kitchen.

"I understand why the dragon-flies are concerned," Lucas said. "All that untrained power. I suspect Sharon doesn't realize the training that you've had, little though it is. She's trying brute force things that would work if you had no training at all, but even basic magical under-standing allows you to avoid those. And with your power… well, she doesn't have a chance. But she's learning. She knew she needed more power and tried to grab Ian's."

"After trying to possess him," I said.

"That may have been to see if I'd catch on," Lucas said. "It would take someone far more powerful than Sharon to possess the Innkeeper, even if he did have spirit magic."

"What if she's draining someone else's magic to augment her own? Darla hasn't been around and we know there's at least one more person, probably two, on the island." Maybe that was why we didn't see the other two. They were lending their strength to Sharon.

"If she's been using it, she wasn't when we went after her. She wasn't nearly powerful enough to have been a spirit with augmented magic. I'm not sure it's possible to link to the living that way."

"What if she possessed someone?" Xavier asked. "If Darla was possessed, would Sharon have access to both her spirit power and Darla's magical power?"

Lucas thought about that. "Darla could work with

another person and have more power. Sharon would be able to guide that if she were possessing Darla. Spirits don't exactly have magical abilities of their own. They have their own power, but they can't work magic. The spirits that are most powerful tend to be the ones who died peacefully, but are back for a specific reason, not directly connected to themselves. Sharon is here for herself, so her power is limited. If Alexander wanted to help you find these people, he'd be far more powerful because it's not really about him."

"Darla didn't have that much magic. I don't think she liked herself much to begin with and got magic because she was just starting to accept herself. Damien brought her to the island, you know," Ian said, setting down another basket of pastries. This one included plenty of berry scones and even two wrapped egg sandwiches. Lucas immediately grabbed one of the sandwiches and opened it. He had his hand in the basket for the other one before I even realized what I was smelling.

Ian, however, noticed that and slapped Lucas's hand and gave me the other sandwich.

I thanked him.

Lucas licked his top lip which had some cheese on it. "You know we need plenty of calories when we're working magic."

"And there's about a million here!" Ian said. "I know Holly appreciates the scones."

"I love those berry scones," I said.

"I also have a few cranberry orange ones, too," Ian said.

Those were my second favorite. I usually picked those in the fall, because the B&B scones had a bit of cinnamon flavoring which made me feel like I was having fall foods.

I'd fallen in love with them shortly after I had arrived on the island.

"Cranberry orange?" Lucas asked. "I don't think I've had those. We tend to have apple scones."

Ian made appropriate noises and the two of them talked scone flavors. I listened while I got my energy back. The food discussion was winding down when Bernice came back into the dining room.

"We have a sheriff's deputy missing from Hidden Rock," Bernice said. "The sheriff got a note that there was a family emergency and the deputy took off. While this didn't raise any eyebrows at the time—things do happen—for some reason my call made the sheriff want to check up on her. He can't get a hold of her and he finally tried calling the woman's brother, who knows of no such family emergency."

"What's her name?" Xavier asked. He'd been relaxed a moment before but now he was ready to pounce on the information.

"Marielle Clouer," Bernice said. "She's tall and thin, short brown hair with a bit of a curl. Last seen wearing blue jeans and a plaid blue and green short-sleeved blouse."

Xavier made notes. "Good observer."

"The sheriff is known for his keen observation skills," Bernice said.

"Which he enhances with a bit of magic to make sure he remembers those things," Lucas added.

"I also talked to the U Council again. They're still working on arranging a visit. For now, they're sending an observer and an enforcer," Bernice said. She's hard enough to read at the best of times, but this time, she was carefully keeping her face neutral. She didn't want people to know what she thought, which led me to believe she wasn't pleased, though maybe she thought everyone would think she ought to be.

Lucas sighed. "Randi Arthur?" he asked.

"Observing only," Bernice said.

Lucas looked down. "She's not exactly on my list of favorite people."

"Who else?" Xavier asked.

"Jeremy Lirai." Bernice looked pleased at that one.

"They aren't messing around," Lucas commented.

"At least Jeremy is someone we can work with," Xavier said. "And they probably figure if Alexander was murdered, then they need someone with plenty of power. Lirai has spirit magic."

"He's a wildcard, though," Lucas said. "Tends to push the boundaries of what he can do…or maybe I should say, should do."

"How long until they get here?" Ian asked.

"They're scrambling for transportation as we speak," Bernice said. "Possibly tonight but maybe not until the morning."

I knew nothing about the people they were talking about. I doubted I could be of any more help and my legs felt strong enough to hold me. In fact, I thought I'd feel better if I moved around, maybe took a walk.

"If no one needs me, I ought to get to work. While we're slow right now, if Jack's gone, I ought to get some things done," I said. I hoped Lucas didn't think I ought to stick around for more training. I might need to move, but I was magically tired.

Ian hurried out to grab a bag. No doubt he'd be sending me across the street with plenty to nibble on. Hopefully, the dragon-flies would let me have some coffee.

I said that to him when he had packed up a bag of scones for me.

Xavier overheard.

"I think we need to test those pods. There has to be a reason the dragon-flies weren't letting you make coffee," Xavier said quietly.

Chapter Twenty-Three

The dragon-flies weren't my only escort over to the accounting office late that morning. Enough people surrounded me that I didn't even feel the chill breeze off the lake, simply because so many bodies were blocking it. The dragon-flies followed, though a few did their flight dance in the air around our group. None of them tried to attack anyone in the group, which I took to be a good sign. I mean, I trusted Ian, Xavier, and Bernice, but I didn't know Lucas.

A red dragon-fly seemed particularly interested in him, though it didn't land on him, it just flitted around his head, causing him to scratch at his scalp a couple of time when the wings got too near and ruffled his hair.

I carried the sack of scones carefully. Ian had a covered mug of coffee, the large travel-size mug for a car, which I hadn't seen him with before. Maybe his magic or the B&B decided to provide me with one to be sure I didn't drink the coffee from the pods.

Inside, the accounting office felt emptier than it

normally did. While Jack usually beat me there, a few times during tax season I worked later or came in particularly early to work on returns. I mostly worked after hours at home, but sometimes I had information at the office that I needed. While the building had felt empty, it didn't feel as empty as it did just then.

This felt abnormal in a way the previous times hadn't. It had to be my imagination, thinking that Jack wouldn't be back.

Xavier had me wait while he, Bernice, and Lucas went to the break room. A few dragon-flies waited with me. A couple hovered near the break room door, looking in at what the others were doing. A few stayed near me and Ian.

Ian handed me the mug of coffee once I set down the scones on the desk. I took it. The dragon-flies fluttered around, but had no issues. Clearly, they were fine with me drinking coffee, just not from the pods in the kitchen.

Bernice came out before I even took a sip from the mug.

"Spelled," she said. "All of them. I'm surprised you didn't notice."

"I was tired this morning," I said. "I didn't sleep well after Lauren's attack. I kept worrying that maybe Darla would show up in my house with whoever was with her."

Bernice nodded. "Perhaps that's why Lauren called you. Either they forced her to make that call or they compelled her to before she understood what was happening. You'd be tired and they could get you to drink the spelled coffee…"

"What sort of spell?" Ian asked.

"Sleep," Bernice said. "Easy enough then to add any other spells to make Holly do what they needed, whether it was a favor to them or to get her off the island."

"Or to keep her sleepy to allow Sharon to possess her," Lucas said. "Sharon might be all about brute force, but she's not stupid."

Lucas was right.

"You can't start practicing spirit magic right now," Lucas ordered. "Doing so has the potential to let Sharon in. You have your guardians for now, but no one knows how long the dragon-flies hang around. You could have weeks or just hours."

I hated that the dragon-flies would disappear again. I quite liked the little things fluttering around.

"Someone suggested that Darla might have gone to the cavern where Damien sacrificed Ann Rogers," I said, looking at Xavier. "If she did, the other people might have gone there too."

Ian looked interested.

"Carl and I have magically searched that area and no one is there. Nothing is out of place."

I wasn't quite convinced. With the dragon-fly effect and all, they could be wrong. They ought to have gone there physically and investigated.

Bernice gave me a long look as I started to press the case that they ought to go there, to look physically. Finally, she turned to Xavier and spoke.

"I think that perhaps the dragon-fly effect could have messed with the results."

Xavier sighed. "Carl is busy with Lauren and for the moment it's just me. Marie just had knee surgery and is still off island. I'll have to wait until Lirai gets here. He can do the search."

Of all the officers, I knew Marie the least. I'd seen her around and heard about her from Carl, of course, but I didn't know her. I'd gotten her taxes done a little early so she could leave and have her knee surgery. I guess that the knee could have been spelled to heal, but as Ian had explained to me, it took a lot of energy and spells might not hold. Marie had more trust in a surgeon and knee replacement, counting on our magic to help her heal more quickly, than she did in a purely magical knee.

From the look on Xavier's face as he had spoken, if I didn't know better, I'd have thought that he seemed reluctant to go searching. Of course, the magic that had been done there had been incredibly negative. Dangerous, even. He'd probably want to stay away. Besides, an outsider was less likely to be fooled by what they might see down there.

Ian put a hand on my wrist and gave me a look I couldn't quite decipher. I wasn't sure if he was urging me to go on my own, to take him along, or to let Jeremy Lirai do the searching.

Xavier held the spelled coffee pods in a bag. "We'll have someone remove the spell at the station," he said. "I don't have that sort of magic, but I want to check them over afterwards. Damien was good at booby-trapping spells. I want to have others around to help if that's the case."

I nodded. I hated that I'd have to go get more coffee. It was probably safer to go out for the next few days. Whoever spelled the coffee pods had gotten into the office. Even if it was Jack, that didn't mean he hadn't left a key for someone else. Or if he'd been possessed, if such a thing was possible, to do these things, he could have been forced to leave a key behind.

Bernice left with Xavier.

"Don't go trying anything," Lucas said. "Sharon is smart and while she's not a powerful spirit, she has humans on her side who could be. I don't like the fact that you're the focus. With two mages who have spirit magic as targets,

I have to believe there's something more behind this than revenge."

Lucas was likely right, although I didn't have a clue what the motive might be. If he did, he wasn't saying. He followed Bernice out the door. I expected he'd probably go to the station to work with Xavier on removing the spells from the pods.

Ian waited. Once the door was closed, he threw his hip out to the right and put a hand on it. "Well?"

"What?" I asked.

"When are we heading down to the cavern? I don't know all of what's going on but things have ramped up over the last few days. I don't like that a spirit attacked me inside the B&B where I should be absolutely, 110% safe and at my most powerful. I mean, maybe it was in hopes of drawing you out, or testing Lucas. Still, I don't know that we have time to wait for Jeremy to investigate. Besides, who knows if he'll think it's important to search the caverns."

My chest fluttered and not in the good way it does if an attractive man flirts from me. This was the flutter of anxiety that comes on when the doctor frowns at you, preparing you for bad news.

"Really? You think we ought to? I don't have that much power and Lucas warned me about trying to use my spirit magic, remember?" I said, looking at him.

"All the more reason to find out now. Sharon isn't a powerful spirit, but we might find out who the humans are. Or I could at least get a fix on them and that could be helpful to Xavier. We aren't going to confront them," Ian said. He made a face. I realized that he was frustrated that his magic wasn't being helpful. He needed to know who was on the island and if his magic wouldn't help him the way it always did, he was going to go there.

"You'll go without me if I say no, won't you?" I said, looking at him.

Ian raised his eyes to the ceiling and then made a sort of questioning smile, "Probably?"

I sighed, my stomach still in knots, but after taking a sip of coffee from the mug, I nodded. "Well, let's get to it."

Chapter Twenty-Four

The last time I'd gone to the caverns, I'd been following Peony. I hadn't had a clue where the little cat was leading me and I'd been shivering with cold and with fear. We'd run through fields late at night and I'd climbed down a short hill towards the beach by the lake in order to find a cave where I could slip inside the caverns below the island.

Ian, however, was an altogether different story. We still had to walk quite a ways because the main street of the town ran along the edge of the island and the cavern was towards the center of the island, perhaps *the* center.

The skies were gray but it wasn't raining that morning. The last time, I'd hit a major storm and had been soaked. If not for the magic of the island I'd have died of hypothermia. A cool breeze hit, but this time I had a jacket and didn't feel uncomfortable. Dragon-flies buzzed behind us, following along, making sure no one attacked, leaving us in a cloud that smelled lightly of clover.

Now and then two purple dragon-flies would flit ahead, like scouts, making sure no one was hiding in the bushes or was about to come running out of a house to attack us. I wasn't sure what the creatures would be able to do if someone did attack, but I wouldn't have counted them out. At the very least, they would have distracted any would-be attacker long enough for Ian and me to use our magic.

We walked along roads, though in many parts of the country these wouldn't count as such. They were wide enough for a single golf cart, but I wouldn't have wanted to have to try passing on the narrow track. It wasn't like Jewel had all that many golf carts around, though. Some houses lined the road, though they weren't close together. One was quite large but most were on the small side, big enough for one, perhaps two people.

Between the houses, bushes and trees lined the road. When we got to a field, surrounded by a fence, Ian slipped into the brush beside the fence line and we pushed our way through the damp leaves and sticky stems of the foliage. A large black horse jogged around the field and it turned to watch us make our way through the trees.

Climbing a slight incline, the trees gave way to a final few bushes and then those abruptly ended, as if someone had planted them and left the rest to be grass. We were in a large field abutting the fenced in pasture. The stallion that watched us could easily have jumped the fence. He'd likely done it before, but today he merely watched us. Once, he'd carried me off to where I needed to go. Today he didn't choose to assist.

Looking around, Ian nodded. "I think this is a good place."

He closed his eyes. My arms began to tingle so hard they started to hurt.

Then it stopped. A square building stood in front of me with two silver doors that met in the center. Having ridden up in an elevator from the caverns before, I knew what those doors would open onto. A small round button with an arrow down sat just to the left of the silver doors.

Ian pushed it. The doors swished open with the same sound a normal elevator makes. He stepped inside.

The elevator looked a bit old-fashioned with shiny dark faux-wood walls halfway up and mirrors on the wall above. The ceiling was industrial white tile and the floor was scuffed and black with a smallish black mat in the center.

I stepped in. Ian pushed the lower level button inside and we descended. The elevator was silent, but either the caverns were very deep or the elevator was slow. It seemed like we rode forever. I couldn't remember if I'd felt as uncomfortable in the elevator I'd ridden up in it or not. Of course, then, I'd been so pleased to be leaving the caverns I probably hadn't cared.

When the doors opened into the cave, the dragon-flies waited for us, swarming around in front of our faces. Four of them landed on my shoulders, three on one side, one on the other. A few breathed threads of fire at us, as if they were trying to drive us back into the elevator.

"Some welcome," Ian whispered.

I understood his reluctance to talk. The elevator hadn't been exactly loud, but the cavern was silent. Ian left the elevator there, though I knew that when we were finished and back above ground, he'd make it disappear.

The dragon-flies were equally silent, except for the buzz of their tiny wings. I looked around the small cave. It wasn't one I recognized. I had to admit that I didn't remember a whole lot about my last hike through the caverns except for a few narrow passages where I worried I would get stuck. I remembered the darkness, but Ian had already created a light and the dragon-flies seemed to glow in the blackness of the cavern.

The light from the elevator poured out into the area

around us, brightening most of the small cave so that only the edges were in shadow. It was in one of those shadows that I finally saw a path out.

"That way?" I asked in a low voice. I didn't whisper as quietly as Ian, but I didn't want to talk loudly either. Who knew where our voices might echo?

Ian nodded after taking a quick look around. There were no other exits except for the way we came in. Ian headed for the path.

"Should we mark the way?" I asked. I wished I had a piece of chalk.

As if reading my thoughts a red dragon-fly flew up and scratched the wall. It scored the rocky wall more deeply than I would have expected from something its size, but then again, these creatures were magic.

"Guess they have us covered," Ian said. He turned and started down the tunnel. I had to follow or be left with only the dim lights of the dragon-flies. While I could have made my own light, I sometimes struggled to keep my fire magic under control. With the dragon-fly effect, I worried that it would get completely out of control and I'd kill Ian or something. I mean, I knew the island should protect him, but that didn't mean he couldn't get badly burned.

This tunnel was low enough that we both had to duck our heads as we walked. I kept an eye on the ground, watching the small stones that covered the ground. Their sharp edges could turn an ankle. I wasn't so young that I could count on recovering quickly and easily. Besides, if we ran into the people who were hiding on the island, I didn't want to be limping away from enemies.

The tunnel turned and became narrower, so much so that I had to hunch over and try and move sideways, my head at an angle. The last time I'd been here, following Peony, the island had made sure I could get through, or maybe that was Peony. This time, it wasn't feeling nearly as helpful. The tunnel was really uncomfortable to walk through and once again I started to worry that there would be a space Ian could get through, but I couldn't.

Not only was Ian thinner than I was, he was far more agile which meant he could probably slither his way through spaces I had no hope of squeezing through. I tried to focus on my breathing but the walls were narrow enough that it was difficult to take the deeper breaths that I normally would have while trying to calm my nerves. At that point all I could focus on was how close the walls were and the fact that my neck ached from the angle at which I had to hold it.

About the time I was ready to scream, the tunnel opened up a bit and then widened even further moments later. The floor sloped down making it seem as if the ceiling had gotten higher. Ian brushed around a poorly placed stalactite that hung from the ceiling. I managed to move around it as well, thankful nothing like that had appeared in the tunnel.

The way opened into a huge cavern. Given the fact that Ian's light didn't reach any wall and just a huge open area filled with stalagmites and stalactites, I figured this must be the cavern where Ann Rodgers had been murdered.

I didn't see anyone at first. Then a shadow moved off to the right. Ian jumped.

The dragon-flies flew towards it. When they got close, their entire bodies lit up like spotlights twice their size and I saw Darla in the shadows.

"Don't hurt me," she whispered.

"Are you alone here?" Ian asked.

"For now. Sharon told Marielle and Clive to go do

something, but I don't know what," Darla said. She sniffled a little bit.

"Please?" she begged. "We have to go now if I'm going to get out of here."

Ian hesitated.

"We should go," I said. "We wanted to find out where they were and now we know. Xavier will have to investigate now."

Darla shook her head. "They're powerful here. Sharon might not have died here, but she spent time with Damien down in this cavern. I was there a few times when they did sacrifices, but I didn't understand what they were doing until too late."

I wondered how you could misunderstand a human sacrifice, but now was not the time or the place to argue with her. While the dragon-flies were keeping her in their spotlight, they weren't attacking or acting as if Darla herself was a danger.

Ian finally decided to leave, taking her with us. He made Darla go first, perhaps assured that the elevator would only work for him if she tried to make a run for it. I went last since we both knew that if Darla was able to move more quickly through the tunnel, I certainly wouldn't be able to catch up with her.

I took one last look out at the large cavern. Behind me, I thought I saw my ancestor, Ann Rodgers shaking her head, looking sad, but when I tried to focus, all I saw were shadows dancing. The dragon-flies urged me into the tunnel, but I couldn't shake the feeling that maybe we were doing exactly the wrong thing.

Chapter Twenty-Five

I managed to avoid breaking my neck as I moved back through the uncomfortably narrow and low-ceilinged tunnel. But it was a near thing. Though it was cool, as always, in the caverns, I sweated through my clothing and my jacket so that I stank of a sickly sweet aroma that reminded me of a terrified animal. Nothing I could do about it, though.

Ian, of course, managed all that without breaking the level of sweat I had. If he was worried, he didn't show it. Darla still sniffled and appeared frightened. I'd have believed her except for the glimpse I'd had of Ann Rodgers in the cavern shaking her head, as if she didn't quite believe the girl.

The dragon-flies continued to hang out around me. Though Darla, too, had spirit magic, none of them flitted around her. In fact, they seemed to avoid her. I wished I could communicate with them without practically freezing to death, but asking about her would be on my list of things to do once I got back to a place where I could warm myself up. Maybe have a hot cocoa waiting. As much as I loved coffee, I knew I'd need some sugar if I were doing anything that drew from my store of spirit magic.

Ian's elevator brought all three of us to the surface. Darla wrinkled her nose, clearly smelling my body odor when I got in the elevator. Ian didn't react to it, almost as if he didn't notice, though I knew he had to have.

Once topside, the stallion, that many said was the heart of the island, waited for us. Not beyond the fencing of his pasture, but right at the doors. He made a grunting sort of snort and pressed his face up to Darla's. She leaned back. I moved around her to stand on the grass. Ian waited nearby.

The elevator disappeared while the stallion was sniffing Darla. He shook his head as if he didn't like something he'd found, but didn't make a move to stop us from taking her to Xavier. As we left, I glanced back to see a few of the dragon-flies hovering around the stallion's head. I wondered what they were communicating.

I paused for a second to watch, but couldn't get a sense of what was going on. The rest of the dragon-fly group hovered close to me. Darla and Ian got further away and when I turned back to follow, I had to hurry and catch up. Fortunately, walks with Bernice meant I was used to moving quickly.

Walking has always been one of my favorite activities. I love walking and seeing things. I can walk quickly when I need to and I rarely tire. People don't believe it of me, usually, though more people here on Jewel seemed to accept that I was a fat woman in reasonable shape. Catching up wasn't all that difficult. When she turned back to see me, Darla seemed a bit surprised to see me. Perhaps she thought the fat woman should have been breathless and struggling. If I were looking for reasons not to like her, perhaps I had found another one. That and the fact that she was loyal to Damien.

"Why did you really come back?" I asked.

Darla didn't bother to turn. "You called and got me fired from my job, remember?"

"I didn't call, but if I did, why come back to Jewel? Did you think I wanted you here?" I asked.

"No. I didn't exactly want to come back, but Marielle made it sound like a good idea. She'd been standoffish at first, like she was suspicious of me, but then Clive talked to her and suddenly she was real friendly."

"Who's Clive?" Ian asked.

"He was one of Damien's students. He left Jewel years ago, before you got here," Darla told Ian. "He knows a ton of stuff about spirit magic. I'm surprised that no one has noticed he's missing given how much spirit magic stuff is going on."

"Bernice called in an expert named Lucas," I said. "He also knows his stuff."

Darla gave a tight smile. "Probably only the acceptable stuff. Not all spirit magic is acceptable. Clive can talk to the dead when he wants to, not just because they come to him."

"You were terrified of ghosts," Ian said. "Do you really want to call up the dead?"

"That's part of controlling them," Darla said. "I can make sure they don't come to me when I don't want to see them. I've been working on it, but I don't have much control yet."

I wasn't sure I believed her about that part.

We pushed through some brush. Darla didn't seem interested in trying to get away from us. She walked along as if we were all friends going somewhere together, though she knew we were taking her to be questioned by the police. There was no way she was innocent of involvement in Alexander Milton's death.

"What about Alexander Milton?" I asked.

"Who?" Darla asked.

"The dead man on the docks," Ian said. "The one who didn't get off the ferry on his own."

Darla sighed. "That was Clive's doing. He poisoned him on the ferry and then animated him until we got here."

"Why?" I asked.

"Alexander had heard some things about Clive. I guess Clive and Damien had managed to do some communicating through spirits. Damien might not have power right now, but Clive was strong enough to get spirit messages to Damien in his sleep. Unfortunately, Alexander had his suspicions and went looking for Clive. Too bad for him. He didn't realize how powerful Clive was."

"Not very powerful to poison someone," I said.

"Powerful enough to make Alexander drink it without suspecting," Darla grinned. As if this was something good.

"You sound like you admire him," I said. "Why come with us?"

"I'm not useful to them anymore. Clive needed a bit more juice to do what he wanted here, but I wasn't useful afterwards. I don't like being cast aside," Darla grinned at me again.

Ian walked along silent, looking troubled. I glanced at him, wondering if he had anything to say, but he only gave a short shake of his head. He timed it so that Darla was looking forward and didn't notice our interaction.

We got to the police station without incident, though I wouldn't have been surprised if Darla's friends had jumped us while we walked. The hairs on my neck prickled more than once, making me turn to see if I were being watched.

Only the dragon-flies were there, flying in formation. Not a one seemed bothered by whatever was making me feel uncomfortable. If I was in danger, I had no doubt they'd be pushing me away from its source and placing themselves between me and said danger.

The skies darkened with a cover of gunmetal clouds ready to burst. The wind whipped itself up in a fury. By the time we'd reached the police station, all the drying sweat on my body had chilled me.

Darla pulled the glass door open and headed into the reception area. Rose was behind the desk, as always. If I hadn't seen her a few times at Derry's, I'd have believed she lived at the station. She always answered the phone, though I suppose with cell phones she could have taken a call anywhere. On the occasions I went to the station, she always manned the desk. While she frustrated me with her slowness, appearing too aged to get the job done, I had to admire her dedication.

Maybe I needed to learn not to judge people. Perhaps the secret shame that Rose had needed to overcome had been getting older, having the shaking head and, sometimes, hands,.

"I'm here to turn myself in," Darla said easily, as if she'd just walked up to a hotel and said she was there for her room.

Rose stared at her, head wobbling atop her skinny neck. I bit back a worry that it would wobble too far and fall off. Finally, she turned and left the desk, perhaps to get Xavier.

Carl appeared. My arms tingled.

"Now, let's have you come back and answer some questions," he said.

Darla found the gate and headed back with him.

I wanted to stop him and ask how Lauren was, what

she had said, but I doubted he'd tell me even if Darla hadn't been there.

Ian started to follow, but Carl held up a hand. "You can wait here if you want, but you can't be there when I question her."

I hated to be left behind when we'd brought her in. "Will we be questioned?" I asked. "We found her in the cavern where Ann Rodgers was killed. She said her friends were coming back."

"If you wait, we can talk after I question Darla," Carl said.

Ian and I headed back to the rickety-looking plastic chairs that sat near the glass by the doors. The reception area wasn't a big place, but then, Jewel didn't normally have a lot of crime. The plastic was cool on my behind, though not cold.

Rain began outside and the wind quickly had it lashing against the glass windows. About the same time, a large ceramic urn appeared near the door, filled with several umbrellas. Dragon-flies popped into the police station waiting area as if they hated the pouring rain.

A late one popped in and dropped onto my lap. Its scales stood up a bit, almost like a cat who'd had a scare. I frowned at it.

"Is that normal?" I asked Ian.

He looked at the dragon-fly. It puffed a bit of smoke, but it was a poor showing. I got the impression it didn't have a lot of energy. Several other dragon-flies crowded around it and started making their tiny little squawks.

Ian held his hands over it. My arms tingled some more. I felt better, but I wasn't sure the little dragon-fly did. It sat there for some time looking wretched. Ian finally stopped and took a breath.

"I've done what I can."

"I feel better," I said. "Almost like you were energizing me."

"Not the intent, but those are dragon-flies so who knows what sort of reaction magic could have when done on them. I don't know that I've ever read about someone trying it."

"Speaking of reading, we ought to check on Lauren," I said.

Ian pulled out his phone and then frowned. "It's not working."

Rose gave us a pointed look and picked up the desk phone, an old black thing that looked like it came out of a 1950s' movie. She listened for a moment and then put it down. She walked slowly across the room, though the way she walked gave me the impression she was hurrying. I could have lapped her four or five times.

Again, I told myself not to judge. That could be me in thirty years. Maybe sooner if I had back problems or if the occasional pain in my hips got worse. I had no problem with Deanna who used a wheelchair around the island. I didn't know why Rose's infirmaries bothered me so much.

Moments later, Carl came out. "The phones are down. It seems to be island wide. I can't even raise Xavier on the radio."

"Do you know where he is?" Ian asked.

"He and Bernice were meeting at her home," Carl said.

"We could go?" Ian said.

"I'd rather you stayed here. Holly has been the focus of these problems and I don't want her out there where she can't call for help. If Xavier has a problem, he can probably let me know magically once he realizes the phones are out."

More rain slashed against the windows.

"It's probably the storm," I said. I knew better though. We'd had storms on the island before and the phones had always worked. The internet and power seemed more reliable on Jewel than anywhere else I'd lived.

"The phones are protected by magic. The island," Carl said. "This isn't from the storm. Either someone found a way to cut them directly or they've used a huge amount of magic to take them down."

There it was again. Someone with a huge amount of magic. On the island.

"Where do they get so much magic?" I asked.

Ian glanced over at me. "If someone is possessing another person, maybe they can access their magic as well as their own. Darla's not that powerful, though."

"Alexander was," Carl said. "Xavier talked with someone about storing magic from those that were murdered as well. It's obscure, but not impossible. Fortunately, like when Damien was cut off from the island, it's short lived."

"Could it be Damien?" I asked. "Could someone be willing to change places in his body and have him out here? Has he got that sort of esoteric knowledge?"

Carl's throat tightened. "I need to contact Xavier. I wish the radios at least worked…" He turned and left.

"Thanks for coming up with an absolutely horrifying idea," Ian said quietly. He raised his eyebrows at me and looked sad.

Chapter Twenty-Six

While the storm raged with no signs of stopping or slowing, the phones came back fairly quickly. I had no idea if magic had worn off, if the person doing it couldn't keep communications down, or if Xavier and Bernice had worked with the island to make sure we had phone use. But my phone jingled not five minutes later. Looking at it, to see if I wanted to answer, I saw it was Jack.

The little dragon fly had flown off after its rest, apparently restored, but I wondered what had happened to make it seem so depleted.

"Jack?" I said into the phone.

That got Ian's attention. He pulled out his phone and pressed it close to mine, probably trying to record everything.

"It's me," Jack said. "I don't know what's going on. Something took over. I was in the dark, not able to do anything. And now I'm in Michigan, in some hotel. It's nice enough but…"

"Get out of there," I said. "Do you have your wallet and stuff?"

"I do," Jack said.

"Then get out of that hotel. Whoever did this knows how to find you there. Go to a different hotel. If you can, rent a car and drive somewhere. Wisconsin would make it easy to get on the ferry when it's safe to come back.

"What's going on?" Jack said. "I'm scared."

"We don't know. We think that you were used to spell our coffee to put me to sleep," I said.

"I remember being in the kitchen…" Jack trailed off before picking up the thread again. "And then I felt odd. I watched myself doing magic, but I wasn't exactly doing it. I went to the docks this morning…"

"I think someone made you go to the hotel you're at. They know where you are if you stay there. If they want to use you again, they'll know where to find you. That's why it's important to find another hotel. Not one that's too close. I'd rather you get as far away as you can."

"Okay." Jack's voice was small.

"I've felt weird for a week now. Do you think…?"

"They may have been working on possessing you," I said.

"But I don't have spirit magic. I didn't think you could possess someone without spirit magic?" Jack said. He whined a bit, as if I could fix that.

"I didn't think so either, so maybe it wasn't exactly a possession?"

"Maybe." Jack seemed primed to discuss this to death. This was the man I worked with. Timid sounding. Willing to dig into the details of everything no matter how unimportant.

"You need to go Jack. Don't even call me for another day, okay? Then call the police department here. Do you have the number?"

Jack didn't. I went up to the counter and got the main

office number. It was unlikely that Rose would be invaded and used. I might find her frustrating but her actions were her own and she put a unique spin on everything. It would be difficult for someone else to mimic her. Even Jack would notice, or at least I hoped so.

Jack wrote it down. I rung off, though he clearly had other questions.

Ian sat frowning. "He's right, you know. He doesn't have spirit magic. Damien wouldn't have had it any longer, either."

"But Clive would. Would he be powerful enough to do something like this?" I asked.

Ian shrugged. "I've never heard of a living mage possessing another. Or course, I've never heard of stock-piling magic by killing other mages, either, but apparently that's happened, too."

"I'm sure that over the centuries most everything has happened," I pointed out.

Ian and I both fell silent thinking about the types of evil that unscrupulous mages might have gotten up to. Rose did her thing behind the desk, whatever it was. She didn't seem to get calls, but she typed away at a computer and watched a monitor. I would have thought of a computer gamer with some people, but Rose didn't seem the type.

Xavier pushed his way through the doors, followed by Bernice and Lucas. Lucas glanced at me and then gestured for me to follow. I got up. Ian did so as well. He wasn't going to be left behind. Considering he was one of my closest friends and I was in the center of this, I didn't want him left out. I couldn't help but think about what had happened to Lauren and I hardly knew her.

Xavier headed back to the office area where he and Carl had desks. Rose watched us go but didn't leave her place at the front desk. Carl was back there with Darla who didn't look particularly pleased to see all of us.

"Have you finished?" Xavier asked Carl.

Carl nodded.

"Good." Xavier sat in his chair. There were two other chairs near his desk. Carl had chairs by his desk and Darla sat in one. Bernice grabbed the other, leaving me and Lucas to grab the two chairs near Xavier. Ian leaned against the wall, probably worried that if he called attention to himself by asking for a chair, he'd be told to leave. As to the police station, it clearly didn't care about the comfort of the people in the building.

"I hear you were working with Damien," Xavier said, looking at Darla.

Darla practically jumped out her chair. Her face went from a slight grin to a frown to something that she probably thought of as a poker face, though I would hope, given the way she reacted to surprise, that she wasn't a poker player.

"I studied with him when he was here," Darla said quietly.

"And now you're working with him," Xavier said.

"I don't know what you mean." Darla looked nervous, glancing at each of us. Her gaze stayed the longest on Lucas. I felt the tiniest tingle of magic and wondered who was working a spell.

"Tell me," Xavier said quietly.

Lucas leaned forward. The tingle on my arms grew stronger.

I watched as Sharon appeared, standing behind Darla, her hands reaching into Darla's shoulders disappearing up her wrists, almost as if her arms grabbed onto Darla's bones. As a ghost, perhaps she did.

Darla sat silent, not saying a word.

Sharon glared at me, her eyes piercing. The dragon-flies who had mostly been flitting around the large room all converged on me and hovered between Sharon and me.

Xavier waved them off, but most ignored him, staying close to me. Others hovered in front of Sharon's face, flitting just above Darla's head.

"What are they doing?" Xavier asked.

"They're protecting Holly from Sharon," Lucas said.

The tingling on my arms began again, getting stronger as Lucas clenched his fists. A dragon-fly squawked at him, but didn't move from where it hovered. Another of the creatures that had been flitting around breathed a thread of fire from behind Sharon.

No one said anything. I watched Lucas work, not certain how much of what he was doing was visible to the others.

A shadow started to flow from Darla's head making it appear that she was growing. Sharon grimaced. I saw her reach behind herself with one hand, searching.

"She's trying to reach either Bernice or Carl," I said.

Sharon's ghostly arm lengthened slightly, nearly grabbing onto Bernice, but the mayor was just a little too fast. Sharon glared at me.

The shadow around Darla's head had grown larger and darker.

Lucas grabbed my hand and ripped my power from me. It clawed through my belly and my chest cutting large swaths through my organs, sheering them off, leaving them ragged and aching. Burning ran down my torso, eating its way from the front of my body to my spine. My back weakened, as if Lucas was taking not just my powers but my bones.

The darkness around Darla grew and then floated off into the clouds.

The dragon-flies surrounded it and each of them breathed their tiny threads of fire against it. Each time they hit the darkness, it dissipated a little more.

Lucas slumped over in his chair and dropped my hand. I felt as if I could sink through the floor, boneless. I must have groaned because behind me, Ian hurried over to the little kitchen area beyond the office. He'd probably work his minor healing magic to wake us so that Dr. Mulrooney or Cassandra could help us further.

"He's gone?" Darla asked in a quiet voice. "How did you do that?"

She looked from me to Lucas, but neither of us was able to speak.

"I could see in Damien's mind what happened. Clive switched places with him and then with me, until Damien could hold my body with me inside," Darla said.

"Interesting," Bernice said. "And you went along with this?"

"Marielle said I'd be defending Damien against the accusations. They'd learned that Holly set him up. I didn't believe it. I mean, I was here. I didn't like what happened. I loved Damien. He'd been good to me, but I knew he was fully capable of doing the things he was accused of. Then I got fired because Holly called my employer and told them horrible things about me," Darla said.

"Who attacked you in Arizona?" Ian asked, bringing two cups of hot coffee, heavily doctored with milk and sugar. I knew those had magic, too. He probably used the sugar and milk to perk us up more physically and his magic to help replenish our stores.

"No one attacked me. They just broke in. I think Alexander Milton had suspicions and he was looking for proof, but he didn't find it in my hotel. It scared me, though, because I thought someone might be building a case against me. I had lent my power to Damien willingly, after all. No one here would allow me to stay on the island because they didn't trust me," Darla said. The whine in her voice suggested that she really believed she was the wronged party. Either that or Darla herself was a far better actor than Damien trying to impersonate Darla had been.

Xavier helped me with my mug. My hands were shaking so badly, I'd probably have spilled it all down the front of my shirt if he hadn't. Ian was practically pouring the stuff down Lucas's throat.

"Clive was on Far Haven's list of watched mages," Bernice said. "Alexander would have been suspicious when Clive made contact with you."

"I didn't know that," Darla said in a small voice. "I mean, I would have helped Damien, but then I learned he wanted to be back here. I think he planned to get Holly off the island and try and take over her body. He and Sharon tried that here, but he hadn't counted on the dragon-flies. Plus, she's learned a lot."

"I made sure she could protect herself," Bernice said drawing herself up. "I wasn't going to let something happen to her again simply because she didn't know her own powers."

"See, that's how Damien treated me when I was new here," Darla said. "You have no spirit magic and didn't understand my magic. But he did. And he cared about me. He taught me all the things spirits could do to me as a mage who could see them. He helped me protect myself."

Bernice nodded. "To your credit, you did believe us, though you defended him at the trial on Far Haven."

"Because he was my mentor. They needed to see that he wasn't all bad!" Darla said.

Lucas took a deep breath in.

Ian picked up my mug and went back to the kitchen.

Chances were he'd be making another cup for each of us. After all, we needed it and a lot more.

"Where are Clive and Marielle?" Xavier asked.

Just as he spoke the dragon-flies started going crazy, flitting around behind me rather than in front of me. They were on the other side of Lucas.

I saw no one where they were flitting, but Bernice stood up, at an awkward angle, as if she were being pulled from her chair. Then Carl appeared to be grabbed by an invisible hand. I felt a chill behind me and Xavier was shoved from his chair, though he nearly fell to his knees. I couldn't see who, or what, was doing it.

Threads of fire erupted from the dragon-flies, these longer than the others, hotter. I felt them even in my seat and wondered if they could always do this or if they saved the fire for real emergencies.

Darla stood and moved backwards, away from what was happening. She wasn't helping anyone, neither us nor our invisible captors.

My arms tingled. Carl said something I couldn't quite understand, but I saw a woman appear behind Xavier, holding him. A man held onto Bernice and Carl, his arms thick. Shadows seeped out of him, almost as if whatever spell made him visible allowed me to see his magic, too.

Even Sharon looked like a normal person to me, although ghosts had always appeared that way. She was trying to help the man holding Carl and Bernice, but as a ghost she wasn't able to do much.

For a moment, I thought the two, who had to be Marielle and Clive, were astral projecting. Then I realized they'd used an invisibility spell. I wondered how long they'd been there and how we hadn't noticed them sooner.

"Damn it," the man swore. He stared at Carl, but he didn't have a free hand. While Sharon placed her ghostly hand over Carl he kept on mumbling words. Sharon muffled his voice, but couldn't silence it.

Lucas looked up. He looked haggard, but he was awake and aware. My body still felt boneless and weak. I could probably hang onto something if they tried to pull me. At least my weight would work my favor in that they couldn't try and carry me, not easily. It would take magic.

The dragon-flies continued breathing fire in the faces of our attackers. The man who must have been Clive screamed at one point and swatted at a dragon-fly. Clearly, he'd been hit.

When the dragon-flies turned to Marielle, she let go of Xavier and covered her face. Unfortunately, before letting him go, she'd cuffed his hands behind him. Still, once freed, Xavier slammed her backwards against the wall. The action sent a shock through the building hard enough that I felt it in my chair.

My arms tingled some more. Someone else was doing a spell. I felt even sleepier than I had. I couldn't quite tell if it was just having had too much power pulled from me too quickly, or if someone was actively trying to put me to sleep.

Clive pushed Bernice into Carl and turned.

Ian stood in the kitchen door. He was the one doing the sleep spell. I fought against it, hoping that his intent would help me stay awake.

The dragon-flies harried Clive but he seemed to understand where they'd be, turning at just the right moment.

I heard one dragon-fly scream. I was reminded of movies where animals screamed before death, the sound cut off abruptly.

I gasped. I had no idea the dragon-flies could be killed.

The rest of the swarm doubled their efforts at breathing fire.

One of the dragon-flies grew larger. A red. The lights in the room glinted off scales as it became the size of a cat and then a large dog.

The fire that came out of its mouth was larger, bigger, setting Carl's desk on fire as it reached out to lick at Clive.

Bernice backed up towards Carl who pulled her to the other side of the desk. I smelled charred wood.

Clive screamed as flames licked at his body.

His hand, which had gotten the worst of it, came away with flesh hanging down, almost as if it had melted in the close contact with the fire.

Sweat beaded on my brow. Lucas' round head dripped sweat.

I smelled nothing but clover.

I turned to see Marielle trying to push Xavier off. He'd pressed a shoulder into her body, holding her against the wall. While Marielle was well-built with muscles clearly defined in her arms, particularly for a woman, Xavier held his own.

I pushed myself up.

"Top drawer," Xavier said. "Keys."

I knew he meant the keys to the cuffs. I took a single step.

The room seemed to turn oddly, but I held myself up, knowing that helping could mean the lives of many of the dragon-flies, as well as my own. I had no idea what sorts of things Clive could call up.

I made it to the drawer.

I saw the keys. My fingers reached for them. Perversely, the keys seemed to skitter away from me. I felt a slight tingle of magic along my arms. Someone was keeping them from me.

I breathed a counter spell.

While the keys stopped skittering around, the room

began to spin. My body was barely holding itself up as it was.

I got the keys.

My legs gave out. I slumped down to the floor, leaning back against the desk. The edge of the drawer caught my blouse.

I held the keys up. Xavier couldn't reach them without leaving his place against Marielle.

Certain I had failed, tears welled in my eyes.

A purple dragon-fly grabbed the keys in its tiny claws. They were heavy enough that it could barely lift them, but it had to go only a few feet. Its flight seemed to take forever, the dragon-fly hardly able to lift itself above the floor.

By the time the little dragon reached Xavier, Lucas had managed to crawl over to my chair and settle himself behind Xavier.

He took the keys from the dragon, which landed on him, resting.

Fumbling a bit, probably from fatigue, Lucas got the cuffs off Xavier.

I exhaled, thinking that was the end of it.

I was wrong.

Chapter Twenty-Seven

Sitting next to Xavier's desk, my arms tingled like a million ants were crawling on them. The tingling never got painful the way it can when someone brings a lot of power, but another colony of ants joined the procession. Perhaps multiple spells. I felt tired, as if someone were trying to make me to go sleep. I figured Ian was still trying to put our attackers to sleep.

Someone else was doing another spell.

As Xavier got Marielle cuffed, I felt a chill. The deep chill that said a spirit was near.

Clive laughed once, an unpleasant bark that suggested he was aware of something no one else was.

Lucas groaned.

I pushed myself over to look at what Lucas saw. Damien shimmered near Darla, a ghost communing with her. Darla had tears in her eyes.

"How?" I whispered to no one in particular. Everyone said Damien was alive on Far Haven, so how was he appearing here, now, looking for all the world like a spirit.

Xavier turned slowly, his back stiff. He looked this way

and that, looking for something. If Damien was a spirit, as I thought, Xavier couldn't see him.

"What is it?" he asked.

"Damien is here. You can't see him?"

Xavier shook his head.

I was right but I didn't understand how it had happened.

"He's dead!" Darla screamed. "You killed him!"

Darla's shoulders heaved as she dissolved into hysterical tears. I watched as Damien's spirit slipped inside her body.

When Darla's tears stopped, her eyes hardened. She studied each of us in turn. I knew that it wasn't actually Darla, but Damien.

My arms tingled again. I was so tired. Xavier sagged a bit. The tingling on my arms grew.

I looked around. Carl and Bernice were throwing spells, whether at Damien or to protect us, I wasn't sure. The fatigue backed off. Now I was merely exhausted from overusing my magic, as if that was any better.

I watched Darla chant under her breath. The small reserves of magic that remained in my body began to drain. The dragon-flies screamed. They breathed fire at Darla and though her nose blackened and the pain must have been excruciating, she didn't move nor did she stop chanting.

I grew weaker.

Bernice and Carl threw more protection spells around us.

"I need magic," Lucas said, his voice a croaking sound. I doubted he had enough energy to so much as light a candle.

But Rose hurried over to him, placing a hand on his shoulder, her old eyes glaring at Darla. Bernice stopped throwing her own spells and stepped over to Lucas, adding her strength to Rose's.

Lucas drew a deeper breath, an agonizing thing that rasped and rattled.

The tingle in my arms turned to an ache which became a fire of pain that ran down from my shoulder to my fingers, as if someone were bathing my arm bones in flame. I bit back a scream.

Xavier put a hand on my shoulder. The ache lessened. I had no idea what he was doing.

"Get out," Lucas whispered.

I felt the magic, felt the pull. Knew Damien felt it too.

But Lucas was weak. Even with the augmentation from Bernice and Rose, he couldn't quite get there.

I shook my head, wishing I had more energy, some power to lend him. But I was a gutted candle with nothing left to give.

Darla laughed.

"Pathetic," she spit. Her voice and the words didn't have quite the same sting that Damien spitting them would have.

Ian hurried over from the kitchen. He had tea with him, which he set down in front of Lucas. He then placed a hand on Lucas' back. Rose moved slightly, giving him more room, which Ian quickly took, stepping into a fighter's stance as if he waited for something to hit him.

I felt nothing so long as Xavier kept his hand on my shoulder.

I noted Marielle watching, waiting for her chance. Even Clive looked hopeful.

Then Damien's expression changed to worry.

While my arms weren't tingling, I felt the earth beneath my feet shudder. The station seemed to tip ever so slightly.

Rose gasped. Her eyes widened.

Bernice looked a little sick.

The dragon-flies almost purred, a low hum that rumbled along like a cat's.

Socrates poked his head around the doorframe. His ears flattened at the sight of Darla. The cat gave a low, menacing growl.

The station, and probably the island beneath it, shook in time with the rumble of dragon-flies. I wondered if they were creating the sensation.

"Get out!" Lucas said. His voice had a bit more force and this time I watched as the spirit that was Damien struggled to keep his hold on Darla's body. The power that Lucas now generated thanks to Ian, was greater than Damien's and Darla's.

Damien, though, held on. As I watched, his hold weakened. Darla's body appeared to shrink, though I knew she hadn't actually changed size.

Carl threw a spell at Darla. Her eyes fluttered. He was trying a sleep spell on her. I wouldn't have thought it would affect Damien, but his spirit seemed to struggle even more. Perhaps Darla's will had been helping hold him in her body.

The land groaned and rumbled again.

The dragon-flies let out a long screech that made the hair on my arms raise and my stomach tie itself in knots.

"Get out, now!" Lucas ordered once again. His voice sounded marginally stronger.

This time, Damien's spirit rose out of Darla's body, still fighting to hold on.

The dragon-flies surrounded her, puffing smoke around her. The smoke drove Damien further from away from her body.

Clive reached out, offering himself to Damien's spirit.

"He's going for Clive." I tried to shout but it came out as a hoarse whisper.

Carl mumbled something. A light shimmered around Clive. He'd heard me.

Damien's spirit hit the light. Bounced off. A protection spell of some sort, then, keeping the spirit out.

With all the magic flying around, I was thankful for whatever it was Xavier was doing to keep me from having to feel the tingling and burning on my arms. I'd have been doubled over in pain by then.

Lucas pointed a finger at Damien's spirit, and it dissolved into nothing.

Lucas' head dropped to the table. Ian stepped back and slumped against the wall. Bernice looked exhausted. Only Rose remained standing, stooped as ever. She picked up one of the mugs Ian had brought and gave it to him.

She gave the other to Lucas and awkwardly helped him drink it, though together they spilled as much as they got down Lucas' throat.

Bernice slumped to the floor, drained.

I felt Xavier's hand leave my shoulder and my head slumped against my chest. I needed rest. And food.

I let my eyes close and I drifted. It might have been only a few minutes or as much as a few hours before I work to feel someone pouring fluid down my throat. This was sweeter than Ian's drink. I swallowed half of it before realizing it was a Dr. Pepper.

Cassandra, our clinic nurse, had arrived and she held the can to my lips. "Keep going. You need the sugars. We've had to use most of our magic on Ian to keep him together. He overextended himself pulling energy from the island. So did Bernice, but she doesn't have the same access that he does."

I took another swig, enjoying the cool, soothing sweetness in my throat. I looked around. We were all still in the police station. Someone had moved Marielle, Darla, and Clive out of the main room. Dragon-flies still flitted around us. Several spit out puffs of smoke, turned, and flew right back through the smoky haze only to spit out more smoke and fly through again, making odd gray patterns in the air.

If I'd had the energy, I would have shaken my head. My back pressed against the wall and pillows surrounded me. I didn't see Lucas nor did I spy Ian.

"Ian?" I whispered before Cassandra got too far away.

"Dr. Mulrooney is with him at the clinic," Cassandra said. "We moved Lucas there, too. The rest of you were just fatigued, though Dr. Mulrooney will be back to check on you as soon as she gets the other two stabilized. Even if we'd wanted to move you, the dragon-flies wouldn't allow her to take you out of this part of the office."

A red dragon-fly hovered between us and puffed a bit of smoke towards Cassandra. She waved a hand in front of her face to clear it.

"That wasn't nice," I said to the creature.

The red dragon-fly turned where it hovered and looked at me. I swear it rolled its eyes at me, though I knew my eyesight wasn't good enough to see something that small.

It went back to staring at Cassandra. She smiled and shook her head before moving over to check on Bernice.

Bernice, too, rested with her back against the wall a few feet away from me. Her eyes were closed and she, too, held a can of Dr. Pepper. I wondered if that brand had more sugar than colas or if they thought Bernice and I were particular fans.

"I am not a fan," Bernice whispered, almost as if she read my mind. She turned her head a little. "I don't like soda in general, but this will pick us up, not just the sugars, but the caffeine. Just don't believe you really have the energy you might think you have. You need to rest. Even more than I do."

"I didn't even do anything at the end," I said.

"Your part came sooner and you were exhausted. Remember that no one works best alone. Even Damien had people he drew energy from. It's best if people share willingly. And then share the burden of the magic," Bernice said. "We worked well together today."

"Is Damien gone for good? I mean, how was he here?" I asked, and gulped down some more soda. Cassandra appeared with another can and a Snickers bar.

I wondered how high my blood sugar would be after ingesting all this stuff. And, faintly, for a just a moment, I worried about my weight. I didn't normally think about it anymore. I had worked hard on accepting my size, but I also didn't eat a lot of sugary things. It had been drilled into me as a younger woman that I shouldn't eat those things, at least not in the amounts that I needed them right then.

"You'll be up for something a little bit more substantial in a bit," Cassandra said. "I need to jump start your energy and while this isn't ideal, it will get us to where you can actually keep down some real food without vomiting."

I pulled the wrapper off the Snickers and bit into the gooey sweetness.

Bernice spoke, though her voice sounded tired. "I believe, though I have not talked to anyone at Far Haven, that Damien must have killed himself and sent his spirit here to possess Darla, perhaps using Clive as a conduit. I expect part of the plan all along was for him to kill himself and then take over a different body. I'd guess he targeted you since you have the most spirit magic. He'd probably have tried doing what he did before but with your powers rather than the island powers. Without magic, though, he needed someone who could possess his body and push him into theirs, which is likely why he needed Clive. Darla and Marielle were just along for the ride, expecting to be rewarded when Damien was back in power."

I bit off another chunk of the Snickers. It really did taste marvelous. And it stayed down without any problems, something I worried about for a moment when Cassandra talked about keeping real food down.

"But he's gone now?" I asked..

"I don't know," Bernice replied. "I don't know how much power Lucas had in those last words. He managed to get Damien out of Darla's body, but that doesn't mean the island is free of his spirit. We may have a bit more work to do."

"Which you can do another day," Cassandra said coming back to us. She took my pulse. Lifted the mostly full can of soda, testing to see how much I'd had. She shook her head a little as if I were supposed to be chugging everything down faster.

"Of course," Bernice agreed, staring straight ahead. I suspect if it were up to her, we'd be out doing that work as soon as we could walk.

Fortunately for me, that wasn't up to her. And we needed Lucas, who was at the clinic.

Chapter Twenty-Eight

I spent the night in the clinic, having been taken there when the others were stable, or stable enough to walk. I'd have been worried about the cats, but somehow they joined me. I didn't feel them come in, but when I woke in the middle of the night to snack on some of the food that had been left for me, Peony was curled up on my legs and Tulip was snoozing curled under my left armpit.

While they normally cuddled from time to time, it was unusual to have both of them curled up with me. I wondered if they were healing me. As I thought that, a stray dragon-fly flew into the room and settled on my chest and began to make the purr sound that I'd heard earlier in the day.

Peony lifted her head to glare at it as if it were stealing her thunder but then she settled back down and stretched, getting comfortable once again. I finished the cheese and crackers and laid back down to get more rest. Looking outside, the darkness suggested that it was still the middle of the night.

After falling back to sleep, I didn't wake again until

Cassandra brought in a tray with breakfast, a huge hearty thing that would take me quite some time to devour. The cats and the dragon-fly were gone. If I hadn't seen the empty plate beside the bed and if I hadn't lived on Jewel for half a year I might have thought I dreamed the interlude, but I knew better.

"How is everyone?" I asked Cassandra, trying to decide where to start on the platter. It held scrambled eggs, sausage, coffee, waffles, and a bit of oatmeal with all the fixings. I picked up a sausage and started with that.

"Bernice went home. She was tired but not completely worn out. Lucas is still here. Dr. Mulrooney took Ian back to the B&B. So much of his power comes from his connection to the building she felt he'd heal faster there than here. She stayed overnight to take care of him in case something happened. It's not often an Innkeeper over-extends himself," Cassandra said.

"I've only just learned a bit about what it means that Ian is the Innkeeper," I said. "But I'm not sure I understand it. I mean how and when does the B&B decide to bond with someone?"

"Usually it's someone with strong hospitality magic. Ian had that, although I'm told that when he arrived he was barely able to do magic. The old Innkeeper here had felt her death coming and the island needed a new person. Ian arrived the day before she…er…died. I guess that there's more commonly about a month of overlap between the old and new Innkeepers. Not having much time with the previous Innkeeper weakened Ian at the start. I have no doubt that was by design." Cassandra made a face.

"Anyway, the B&B has taught him what it can. I know Bernice is thinking about bringing someone to help teach him more, now. I doubt anyone really thought he'd overdo it like he did, but he's a people person. I also think he's watched what you've done and figured he could be just as helpful. I have no doubt Bernice is not pleased by that example, but we all do what we have to do. Another Innkeeper will help keep Ian aware of what exactly his limits are."

"I hate that Ian could have harmed himself trying to help me," I said.

"He was helping all of us. We don't need Damien trying to take over the island again. If not for you, we'd all still be under his thumb. Damien's not a foolish man so I expect if he'd taken over a body, he'd have hidden himself well," Cassandra said. "And by the time people figured it out, it would have been too late. Fortunately, the fact that they just left Alexander Milton's body on the dock gave us a head's up."

"I heard that they drugged Alexander and then Clive, possessed by Damien, killed him while he was still drugged," I said.

"I heard that, too. I'm not sure why Clive didn't leave the body on the ferry after killing him," Cassandra said. "The only thing I can think of is that Alexander died fighting to keep Damien from trying to possess him. Damien probably didn't realize that he wouldn't have Clive's full powers, nor do I expect he realized how powerful Alexander really was. I have heard that there are spells to animate a dead body. If anyone knew how to do that after death, it would have been Alexander. Maybe he managed to move his body off the ferry."

I chewed thoughtfully.

"I need to go check on Lucas and you need to eat," Cassandra said. "I'll be back with coffee in a few. It's spelled this morning, so it should perk you up faster than usual."

"How's Lauren?" I asked before Cassandra could shuffle off.

"She's still sleeping, but it seems lighter. I expect she'll wake any time now. I hope that the spell doesn't keep her from remembering what went on."

As Cassandra left on nearly silent feet, I tucked into the waffle. I'd leave the eggs for last. I had a feeling if I ate all of them I might be overdoing it. It seemed like they'd scrambled a dozen just for me.

As I ate, I felt stronger, better. I wasn't as fatigued and the slight fogginess in my head and the vague ache between my eyes went away. I had a certainty about being able to do small types of magic that I had lacked before.

Cassandra came back when I'd finished the tray. As promised, she had more coffee.

"Dr. Mulrooney will be back in a few minutes to check you over. I expect you'll be cleared to go home."

"So Ian's okay then?" I asked.

"Not as good as you, but he pushed further," Cassandra said. "I'm not sure he knew where his own reserves ended and the B&B's began. It's something that Bernice will make sure he learns."

I wanted to see him, but he was at the B&B so I needed to wait at least until Dr. Mulrooney released me. It was hard. No dragon-flies came and kept me company nor did my cats mysteriously appear in the room. All my magical friends were leaving me alone.

Finally, the doctor arrived. My arms tingled as she gave me a magical once-over. Then she moved on to the purely physical examination and finally declared that I could go home.

"I don't care what Bernice might think. You need to rest right now. They have investigators from the U Council here, too, so you shouldn't be immediately needed," Dr. Mulrooney said. She gave me a stern look.

I nodded, glad to be going home. When I left the clinic, Xavier was waiting for me in a golf cart, ready to take me there.

"Wow, what service," I said.

"Cassandra doesn't want to leave Lucas and Lauren," Xavier said. "Dr. Mulrooney will be heading back to the B&B and Ian. Honestly, with Lucas, they're more worried about possession than anything."

"Like Damien might have possessed him?" I asked.

"That or that Damien might try now that Lucas is so weak. The investigators have put spells down, the sort that most people don't know, although Clive was a sneaky one so he might have figured those out. That would be the first step in learning to subvert them."

I hadn't heard about subverting spells, but it made sense. After all, nothing was fool-proof.

The golf cart putt-putted along with the two of us inside. Xavier didn't say much more. I bit my lip, worried about Lucas. What if he had been possessed and no one noticed. I didn't know how someone would figure out if another person was possessed. Lucas was supposed to be teaching me those things, but how could I ever trust that he was really Lucas and not Damien?

Logically, I knew that others would test him and use magic to find out if he were himself, but I'd seen Damien work. He was subtle and he was smart. He had to be to do what he'd done. I hated not knowing if he was really gone.

Chapter Twenty-Nine

I got to rest for two more days, although I spent way too much time worrying about whether Lucas was really Lucas and not Damien. I talked to Randi Arthur and Jeremy Lirai for hours the second day. They interviewed me in one of the back rooms of the library.

I didn't know about the door to that side of the building until I got there. The main door was locked and we had to go around to the side. Always something new to learn on Jewel, even about the library.

Randi told me the library room was more private than other places, but not as official as the police station. The mention of the police station surprised me, and I worried that perhaps they thought I had something to do with what had happened. However, none of their questions implied that I was a suspect in any wrong doing.

I also hated that I worried about being a suspect because Jeremy Lirai's dark good looks were easy on the eyes. Maybe he got where he was because everyone wanted to tell him things, hoping for the spark of light that came and went behind his eyes whenever something pleased him. I'd have told him anything to see that. It wasn't until later that I wondered if it had been a subtle spell, though my arms hadn't tingled.

After talking to them, I finally got to look in on Ian. I found him at a table in the B&B's dining room. He looked pale and wan and he'd lost weight, though if the spread in front of him was any indication, he was eating well. He also didn't have quite his usual level of playfulness, seeming a little bit depressed.

"Still getting my mojo back, I guess," he said, giving me an almost smile. I hated seeing him like that. Even after fighting Damien the first time, Ian had managed to bounce back much more quickly than this.

"I heard you're getting your own teacher soon," I said.

"Not for a month," Ian said. "Bernice made a bunch of calls, but the senior-most Innkeepers all wanted me to go there and she wasn't about to let me leave right now. I think she's worried if I do, I won't come back."

Given the way he wouldn't look at me when talking, I worried about that too. I wondered what could have gone on that left him feeling so damaged.

The next morning was Saturday and I had barely had my coffee and some toast when the phone rang. The dragon-flies, which had been flitting around outside my home every day since I'd returned, were suddenly in my dining area, as if I needed protection from the caller.

Maybe I did.

It was Bernice telling me that I was needed at the police station as soon as I could get there. I glanced out the window, noting that sky was clear. Still, having done battle before, I worried that I'd need a sweater so pulled one on.

Peony and Tulip both came out to the living room and

watched me leave, almost as if they were saying good-bye. A hard knot formed in my stomach.

I felt like a prisoner on death row heading for the executioner. That analogy did nothing to make me feel better and I tried to push it from my mind. Of course, the harder I tried to do so, the more the thought hung on.

By the time I got to the police station, I was ready to throw myself down and say, "Just get it over with!" Not that anyone else would have known what I was talking about. Which was probably fortunate. I didn't need everyone to know how stressed I was.

Lucas was already there and he looked pale and drawn. Unlike Ian, he didn't appear to have lost weight. Xavier looked stressed. I swear there were new lines on his face.

Carl looked stoic, which is to say he looked much like himself. Bernice held herself tall and straight, as still as a stone, which was also normal for her.

Randi Arthur sat on the edge of Xavier's desk, her foot moving back and forth. She had her bleached blonde hair trimmed short around her face, her pale gray eyes tracked everything. The faintest tingling in my arms told me she was using a spell, though she kept it very low key. I wondered how many other people were as sensitive to magic working as I was.

Jeremy leaned against the wall where Ian had stood the other day. His nearly black hair and the rugged planes of his face gave him a movie star handsome quality, at least to my mind. He was built like a linebacker and I'd heard rumors that he had played in college, though it was a smaller one. This morning, his dark eyes held no warmth in them, ready for anything to happen. I suppose it would have been too good to be true if a man as smolderingly sexy as him was interested in me.

Not that a woman couldn't hope. I might have been

nearly menopausal, but I wasn't dead. In fact, from what I had read, at my age, I was just coming into my sexual peak. Which made the fact that I spent most of my time with a young gay man all the sadder.

"So we're all here," Jeremy said quietly. I hated that they'd been waiting for me. I mean, Lucas had been weaker than I was and he still looked it.

Lucas cleared his throat and started to speak. He sounded hoarse.

"I managed to get Damien out of Darla's body. We've had multiple different protection spells around her and Clive while they were on the island. We called in help from the enclave in Kentucky to take them off island," Lucas said quietly. "Damien's spirit is definitely still here though. No doubt that was a huge part of his plan when he killed himself."

"He had Clive carry him here by changing bodies. When Damien jumped into Darla's body from Clive's, Darla didn't have the power to jump into his body in Far Haven. When Damien didn't go back, his body fell into a coma almost immediately. All vitals ceased yesterday morning. We know that prior to the death of his body, Damien had used Darla's body for short periods of time."

Lucas paused to clear his throat and take a sip of tea that smelled not unlike the tea that Ian made when I was fatigued.

Jeremy jumped into the conversation. "In interviewing her under the strongest truth spells I've got, Darla seemed conflicted about holding Damien's spirit. On the one hand, she seems to worship him. On the other, she didn't want to be involved in harming anyone. She didn't mind being the one to lead someone to another person who would hurt them, but she didn't want to do the dirty work herself."

Bernice's frown got just a little deeper. A huge tell for her.

"I wasn't able to get rid of Damien altogether," Lucas said. "He's not a mage, but someone put some sort of protection spell on him as a spirit. I suspect it was Clive, but he hasn't admitted to anything. We need to find where Damien is on the island and banish him."

"It's probably the cave," I said. "The cave in the center of the island where we found Darla. It's also where Damien killed the women he used to give himself magic."

"That was our thought," Jeremy said. "Unfortunately, none of us knows where the cave is."

All eyes turned to me.

"I followed the calico cat the first time. It seemed like a cave opened on the cliff on the far side of the island. The second time, Ian took me using an elevator. It was how he rescued me," I said.

"I can do the elevator," Bernice said. "Do you remember where you were up top?"

"Approximately," I said. I worried that sending an elevator down the wrong space would trap us there. But the island wouldn't let that happen. Besides, if the doors opened to rock, they'd probably just close again and we'd ride back up to the surface. At least I hoped things would work that way so we weren't stuck in the middle of the earth.

"Then let's go," Jeremy said.

Lucas pushed himself to his feet, slowly. He didn't groan but it looked like he wanted to. I moved aside so everyone could get out of the office. Once we were in the parking lot, the dragon-flies joined me. They followed us, but hung behind. I walked more slowly than I normally would have so that Lucas could keep up. Bernice stayed a few steps ahead, pausing now and then to let us catch up. She wasn't able to slow down as much as was needed.

Xavier held Lucas' arm. I worried that Lucas wouldn't be up to fighting off Damien. I wasn't sure how much strength I had. I looked over at the golf carts but no one else seemed to notice them. Perhaps walking was good for us after using our magic. A nice walk often was, though this was not exactly what I would describe as nice.

Randi and Jeremy didn't seem particularly worried.

"Will Lucas be up to this?" I whispered to Bernice when we got a bit further ahead again and had to wait for the others.

"He has to be," Bernice said. "I can lend him my strength. He can also guide you if need be. That will be easier on both of you if you take point and can force Damien to leave the island. The island likes you. It doesn't know Lucas other than as another mage. You, it has forged a friendship with if the dragon-flies are any indication."

"Are the dragon-flies a manifestation of the island?" I asked.

"No one knows," Bernice said quietly. A shrug would have offered too much insight into what she thought. We continued walking across the island, Bernice, Jeremy, Randi, Xavier and I, with Lucas bringing up the rear. I wished Ian were here, but I knew he was still too weak and not fully recovered.

"Ian looked as if he'd lost weight," I said.

"He has," Bernice said. "He far over-extended himself. Not something you want to emulate. He's only alive because he's the Innkeeper and the island won't let him die from over-extension. He's basically living on magical help from the island until he can get his own magic and strength back."

Another thing I didn't know. While the island protected

us, it did not protect us from ourselves. If I were to overdo it and exhaust myself unto death, the island wouldn't stop me.

"I know that you have a connection to the island as mayor. Will it protect you?" I asked, keeping my voice low.

"Not like it does with Ian," Bernice said. "A mayor is elected by the people. The Innkeeper is chosen by the island. Naturally, the island favors the one it chose, not that it dislikes me or anything. It looks to me to see what people want in the same way it looked to Sharon when she was elected. We represent the people to the island magic as well as in the government."

It made sense to me. I was glad that the island was taking care of Ian, but I still worried about him.

By the time we got to the place where Ian had created an elevator, I felt warm in my sweater. The sun was high in the sky and I didn't see a single cloud.

Bernice looked around, waiting for everyone to get there. Lucas was nearly limping when he got there and his face was paler than it had been. So much for a nice walk being good for us, although I did feel energized.

"Are you going to be okay?" Bernice asked.

"I can guide Holly," Lucas said.

"And I can lend strength," Jeremy added. "Randi can ground us to be sure no one over-uses their magic as they did the other day."

My arms tingled as Bernice wiggled her fingers in the air and an elevator appeared. Hers was a bit more upscale than Ian's with a shiny black interior and red and black carpeting on the floor. The lights were even and well maintained. Once we were all inside, and we all fit, she pushed the down button.

I felt the slightest whoosh as we descended and moments later the door opened onto the exact large cavern where I'd found Ann Rodgers' body. Apparently, my memory was still reliable.

The cavern was chilled and I'd barely stepped out before something rushed at me. The dragon-flies popped in and started spitting fire at the spirit, causing it to pause.

Damien had been waiting for us.

Chapter Thirty

The huge cavern smelled of rotting garbage. That was different. The air was cooler than I remembered. While I'd been freezing the first time, I'd not been too uncomfortable the last time. Of course, spirits always made places cooler.

When I see spirits, I see what looks like a real person. Damien was pale with dark hair and a long thin face of the sort that could have played a TV villain or perhaps a vampire. I'd even worried he might be a vampire when I'd first come to the island. Instead, he was something other, though just as dangerous. Perhaps more so.

He wore a black outfit. I wondered if that was his preferred outfit or if that had been what he was wearing when he died on Far Haven. It might have been a foolish thing to waste time wondering about, but while I was getting used to magic and spirits, it wasn't every day that I had to confront one.

The dragon-flies continued to breathe their tiny threads of flame which kept Damien at bay. The stink of garbage was soon subsumed by the smell of burnt clover.

"He's here," Lucas said.

I felt his hand on my shoulder. Power flooded through me.

Bernice took my hand in hers, her skin papery dry, feeling older, almost frail in a way I never associated with her.

Two others reached out and placed hands on my back, probably Xavier and Jeremy. The power flooded through me.

"Focus on the spirit," Lucas said, his hoarse voice low. I had no idea if he was too weak to speak more loudly or if he wanted to keep Damien from hearing.

I breathed in, staring at Damien, holding his eyes. The dragon-flies continued to flit and whirl between us.

"When you tell him to leave, tell him to go to his final resting place and never return. Think about locking him in that place. Picture a cell or a coffin with chains on it. Whatever works for you," Lucas continued. "Put all the power you can behind it. He's strong. He might not be a mage, but he was a strong personality in life and he remains so in death."

I settled myself, focusing first on my breathing, though I kept my eyes on Damien's. They'd always been dark eyes, but now they were black pits, waiting to subsume me. I felt myself being pulled in, spinning like I was falling into a whirlpool of midnight water.

The hand on my shoulder pulled me back.

"Stay in control," Lucas hissed.

I pictured a cell. I had no idea what cells looked like on Far Haven. The image that came to my mind was an old-time jail cell with bars on all sides and a solid earthen wall on the back. The floor was earth, and I pictured boulders beneath it. Bars were on a long narrow window.

"Leave and go to your final resting place!" I ordered.

I sent the energy that I filled me out through the order,

pretending that my voice threw actual objects across the room towards the spirit. The dragon-flies moved out of the way the moment I opened my mouth to speak.

I felt the chill of Damien's spirit trying to access me and, through me the magic. I felt someone unwrap the tangled magical cords he tried to wrap around me.

"Leave us and go to your final resting place!" I ordered again. I pictured him being pushed back towards the cell, as if we were herding him into it. In my mind, I saw him being pushed inside, but he held onto the bars, refusing to be forced into the cell.

My heart thudded. My arms felt shaky.

I was using a lot of power but Randi hadn't stepped into say anyone was overdoing it. That was her job this time. I could keep pushing him.

The dragon-flies flew in front of me. Two landed on my head, a scratchy crawling feeling that I didn't like, though the soft croon of their almost-purr was comforting and strengthening.

"Go!" I shouted, putting all the force I could muster into it. I infused the command with the anger I felt at him nearly murdering me, the devastation I felt at having been part of killing Sharon, a woman I had liked, the anger and anguish I felt at not having Ian by my side. I drew all the magic I could muster.

Damien's spirit tumbled backwards into the cell. Mentally, I slammed the cell door and locked it.

He rattled the bars. I put magical wards on them and made sure the bars were the strongest metal I could imagine. His cell morphed in a sort of science fiction image of force fields and heretofore unknown metals that would hold the strongest of evil creatures.

Damien's spirit glared at me.

I felt someone else doing magic. The image solidified and got smaller, like it was being made into a cube.

Lucas's hand dropped from my shoulder. I felt him slumping against me.

The dragon-flies squawked around him. The two on my head left to check out what was happening. Others flitted around where the cube was getting smaller and smaller.

"One more time," Lucas whispered, so low I wasn't sure I really heard him. "Send him to his final resting place."

"Go to your final resting place," I ordered, giving it all my authority. I rarely had to discipline my nieces and nephews, but now and again they got overly rambunctious. I put that same tone that brooked no arguments into my voice. It was the authoritative tone I had used to tell Jack to flee when he'd found himself off the island.

The cube flickered once and was gone.

The dragon-flies looked back at me and spun around and spit small puffs of smoke in my face. I slumped a bit, but several hands kept me from falling. Having power from others made the confrontation easier than I had expected. Bernice was right about working with others.

I should have known.

Chapter Thirty-One

I managed to get to the clinic on my own. There I was fed and given plenty of liquids. Afterwards, Dr. Mulrooney insisted I go to the B&B to recover so someone could make Ian, Lucas, and me plenty to eat all at one time. We were all ambulatory enough to make it to the dining room.

Which meant that later that evening I sat at a table for four pushed against the wall with Ian beside me and Lucas across the way. We all had full plates of the tenderest steak I had ever eaten, baked potato, and plenty of chewy bread which we slathered with butter. The salad we'd had earlier could have been a meal all on its own on a normal day.

"This is good," Lucas said, stuffing some bread into his mouth as if he hadn't eaten for a week.

Ian nodded, hardly pausing as he shoveled more steak into his mouth. I didn't even see him chew.

I ate more slowly, but I'd been less over-worked than either of the two men. However, just because I ate a bit slower didn't mean that I wasn't stuffing myself every few hours.

"The island feels better," Ian said. "Before, there was a

sort of grayness to everything, like a fog was starting to come up. Now it feels more normal again."

"Jack came back on the evening ferry," I said. "Xavier and Bernice examined him for over an hour and he appears to be normal now."

"Good," Ian said. "Jack may not be my best friend on the island, but he's Jack and I would hate for him to have been tricked into helping someone like Damien. He is rather naïve about people."

"That was a neat trick of Clive's. I'd love to learn how he did it, but he's not talking," Lucas said. "I can backtrack the magic when I feel better, though. There should be some lingering about. So long as the dragon-fly effect doesn't erase stuff faster."

As if speaking of them, one of the dragon-flies appeared in the dining area and flitted around.

"Pretty purple," Ian said, looking at the tiny creature. The coloring was lovely. Ian held out a hand, but the dragon-fly ignored it and settled on my shoulder, the one nearest the wall. It spit a bit of smoke at Ian.

"I'd say it doesn't love you that much," Lucas said, chuckling a little.

The dragon-fly blew smoke at him, too.

"I would love it if they loved me as much as they love you," Ian said.

"I've never known any dragon-flies to like someone as much as they like Holly," Lucas said. "I think it's worth studying."

"They seem like they're linked to the island's magic." I dug my fork into my potato to scrape the skin for a bit more. "Is that always true? And are the enclaves all one magic or are they separate, more like individuals?"

"They're all connected, of course, but each enclave has a personality and it's not just from the people there. It's a joining, like Ian and Inn, with the spirit of their making and the magic. I'm sure the right people are drawn to the proper place, but everywhere I've gone there's been a different feel, even to the magic." Lucas put down his cup.

Ian looked thoughtful. "I wonder if I could tap into the magic of another enclave?"

"You'd have your own magic and the link here. If you tried drawing from another enclave the way you draw from here, you'd be cited," Lucas said. "It's been tried."

Ian looked interested, but didn't pursue the conversation.

"Are Darla, Clive, and Marielle going to be taken to Far Haven?" I asked.

"Clive and Marielle are." Lucas said before taking another bite of steak as quickly as he possibly could. I was surprised that he didn't pick up the slice of meat in his hand and just chew on it. When he glanced down at it again, I figured he was probably wondering the same thing.

"Darla will be going to Forgotten Key," Ian said. "It's got a prison, but it's minimum security. She won't have access to her magic or be able to leave, but she can live in an ordinary home rather than a cell. They do some rehab there as well and maybe the psychologists she'll be working with will be able to determine how much she was willingly helping and how much she was forced or spelled to help."

I'd have loved to have an answer to that last question. Darla had tried playing both sides far too often for me to feel really comfortable believing that she hadn't been willingly involved.

"Jack will probably have to go see Xavier and Carl weekly to be checked for any influencing spells and also have an examination by a U Council psychologist who will be here soon. If you liked Jeremy, you'll love him," Ian said nodding in my direction.

My face heated. I had no idea if Ian actually knew I was attracted to Jeremy, or if he'd been attracted to him and had decided I'd feel the same. Jeremy, unfortunately, had left us without so much as a farewell. Not that it mattered. It wasn't as if there was any chance of a long term relationship with someone who rarely came to the island.

"And you?" I threw the comment back at him.

"Oh yeah," Ian said. "I'll be looking. He'll be staying here, so I'll get to talk to him all the time." He smiled as he broke off a hunk of bread and chewed, eyes half-closed.

"He was here before," Ian said finishing his bite. "I think three or four years ago when Mindy got in trouble at Derry's. She was using magic to inflate bills by a few cents here and there."

I nodded, thinking about how Sharon had warned me about Mindy pushing limits when I'd first arrived.

"Anyway, he spent a month on the island and Mindy's not done it again, though they monitor her regularly, especially her tips," Ian said. "Not that you need tips here because everyone gets a decent base salary."

He was right. It was one thing I liked about Jewel. My condo had chosen me and there wasn't a cost. I made enough to afford my other living expenses and put some away. When I'd worked overtime during tax season, my bank account had accumulated money faster than I thought possible.

Almost like magic.

If I wanted, I could work doing things around the community to earn a bit extra, too, but salaries—all of them—were decent and allowed people a place to live and food to eat. The basics.

Just as we were finishing, Dr. Mulrooney brought Lauren in. Her eyes were somewhat sunken and her face pinched.

"She's doing okay," Dr. Mulrooney said. "She ate lunch earlier and she's still awake. She wanted to see you all."

Lauren settled in at a chair, next to me, facing the two men.

A large flurry of queries into her well-being assaulted her as she sat. Lauren smiled at all of us. Dr. Mulrooney slipped out while we were all trying to get Lauren's story.

"I'm okay, now. I think that the sleep spell was just really strong and the dragon-fly effect made it last longer."

"Why did you call me instead of calling Xavier immediately?" I asked.

"It felt right at the time," Lauren said. "I think it was sort of the sleep spell. Everything felt like a dream, but I was still moving. The library had to step in and protect me."

"How bad is the mess?" Ian asked.

"I haven't even looked," Lauren said. "I know that just about every book off the main shelves flew at Darla and the woman with her. They ran out pretty quickly. It'd have been funny if I'd been awake enough to enjoy it. Of course, if I'd been awake, the library wouldn't have had to fight them off for me."

"I'm glad it did," I said. And I meant it. Lauren was smart and she was good at answering the questions I came up with, and didn't make me feel foolish for not knowing things. She might be more reserved than Ian, but I'd come to enjoy her company a great deal.

"Me, too," Ian said, when he finished gulping down some fruit juice that remained on the table. "And I can probably help with the clean-up, assuming you don't need magical help."

"I can probably do some spells," Lauren said. "I need to get the place reopened. I know not everyone uses it all the time, but when the library is needed, it's really needed."

"I had no idea the building would come to your rescue," I said. "Are all the buildings like that?"

Lauren shook her head. "Just the library. And it's really protecting the books, but they know that if the librarian isn't around, they'll be locked up and the magical books don't like that. The library thrives on people's energy."

Another tidbit I hadn't known. Not that it mattered much now. I was just glad Lauren was okay.

After we chatted for a few minutes, Edie brought out a huge platter of cheese and fruits. We'd have desserts with sugar later on.

We all picked at the cheese and the grapes, even Lauren. Ian put some of the brie on the bread that seemed to be never-ending. The basket was probably spelled so it didn't run out. There were many things to love about Jewel.

And who knew. Maybe Ian would be right about the psychologist. Even if I never found a love, I was pleased with life on the island. For now, I was especially pleased that Damien was gone. This time for good.

The purple dragon-fly on my shoulder puffed out a bit of smoke. It grabbed at the grape I was about to pop into my mouth and stole it from me.

Lauren laughed, which drew Ian's attention. Even Lucas gave a loud guffaw. So much for the dragon-flies liking me best. But since it made us all laugh, something none of us had been doing for some time, it was a good thing and perhaps the creature's whole goal.

Things were looking up.

About Bonnie Elizabeth

Bonnie Elizabeth could never decide what to do, so she wrote stories about amazing things and sometimes she even finished them.

While rejection stung her so badly in person, she spent most of her young life talking to cats and dogs rather than people, she was unusually resilient when it came to rejections on her writing, racking up a good number of them.

Floating through a variety of jobs, including veterinary receptionist, cemetery administrator, and finally acupuncturist, she continued to write stories.

When the internet came along (yes she's old), she started blogging as her cat, because we all know cats don't notice rejection. Then she started publishing.

Bonnie writes in a variety of genres. Her popular Whisper series is contemporary fantasy and her Teenage Fairy Godmother series is written for teens. She has been published in a number of anthologies and is working on expanding her writing repertoire.

She lives with her husband (who talks less than she does) and her three cats, who always talk back.

Find her at www.bonnielizabeth.com

Stay in Touch

Taken by the Sound

An Air of Suspicion

Little Dog Lost

Death Interrupted

Down in Whisper

A Haunting Whisper

A Haunting Attraction

Secrets Not Whispers

Only Human

Other Novels

One Bad Wish

Sun Spot Magic

Ghosts from the Past

Unnatural Secrets

Shadows of Solstice

The Haunting of Steely Woods

Find them all at your favorite bookseller or check us out at
MyBigFatOrangeCat.com